# The Queen of the Hills

To Mary
with love
Merton Oaten

Copyright © M. Oaten, 2005

First Published in 2005 by
Serendipity
First Floor
37/39 Victoria Road
Darlington

All rights reserved
Unauthorised duplication
contravenes existing laws
British Library Cataloguing-in-Publication data
A catalogue record for this book is available from
the British Library
ISBN 1-84394-173-2
Printed and bound by Antony Rowe Ltd

# The Queen of the Hills

Marian Oaten

# Chapter 1

One windy morning in late November 1913, Dorothy Ollis was making her way towards Victoria College, as was her wont. She was the second daughter of a Welsh teacher who had moved to London. She considered it a great stroke of luck that at the end of her schooling she had been taken on as the private secretary of the Principal of the college, one which had a high reputation in the academic world. When Dorothy was nearing the end of the somewhat lengthy drive, she heard the noise of a cab approaching rapidly. It came to a halt on the space in front of the college entrance amidst a crunching of gravel. Meanwhile Dorothy too had arrived at the entrance and saw Miss Clare Davies, the Principal, waiting there. The door of the cab opened and out of it stepped an imposing female figure. The lady hastened forward to embrace Miss Clare.

'How is papa?' she said. In anguish Miss Clare answered, 'I'm afraid there's little hope.'

Clare turned towards Dorothy and taking her by the hand introduced her to her sister, Gwendolyn Waterhouse, just arrived from India, where she had been living for many years. Then turning to Gwendolyn she introduced her to Dorothy, describing her as her faithful secretary and friend. After that the ladies made their way to Clare's study, where tea was waiting for them. While they sipped it, Gwendolyn said, 'My husband didn't really want to let me come on my own, as the voyage is too long; but in view of papa's frail state of health, I rather insisted on coming all the same.' Clare interrupted to explain to Dorothy that Gwendolyn's husband, Major Liam Waterhouse, was advisor to the Governor of Bengal and lived in Calcutta. Gwendolyn went on to tell stories about the life on board ship and the people she had met during the long month of the voyage. When the conversation was over and Gwendolyn had recovered a little from the fatigue of the journey, she asked her sister where she would be staying and if she could see her father at the earliest possible moment.

'Naturally you will be staying in the college guest room,' answered Clare. 'As for papa, I hope to be able to take you to see him in the hospital tomorrow.'

Clare rang the bell, and shortly afterwards Gladys the maid appeared. She showed Mrs Waterhouse to her room so that she could unpack.

Victoria College was founded around the end of the nineteenth century to meet the pressing demands for higher education for women. It formed part of London University, though it was built at Egham, well outside the capital near the River Thames in an area of green fields and woods. From its start Victoria College gained an enviable reputation both for its academic standards and the sporting achievements of its students. The first Principal, in fact, was Annette Webb Ellis, the granddaughter of William Webb Ellis, who invented the game of rugby, and like him was keen on sport. At the same time she was a scholarly lady. Miss Clare Davies put all her effort into keeping up the reputation of the College, making it ever more difficult for students to gain entry to it with its stiff entrance examinations. Dorothy was proud to be a part of this great establishment, though she would have preferred to attend the courses as a student, but the financial circumstances of the family had ruled that out. So she had welcomed the chance offered by Miss Clare to be her personal secretary, a job that she had now been doing for three years.

Gwendolyn was a representative of the upper echelons of Anglo-Indian society, and her arrival introduced a fresh breath of novelty into the academic rigidity of the college. Christmas was not far off, and Gwendolyn, with her lively mind, suggested to her sister and Dorothy that together they should organize a concert for charity (the beneficiaries being abandoned Indian children), given by the students that had artistic talents. Dorothy welcomed this idea with enthusiasm and immediately volunteered to perform on the piano. A date was soon fixed for auditioning the various offerings of the students. Even Clare at this point began to get keen on the idea, though with a certain degree of hesitation.

The Queen Charlotte Hospital at Egham was not far from the college and offered every assurance of care and attention; which was why Clare had chosen it for her father to spend his days in as

# Chapter 1

comfortably as possible. The tumour that he had been diagnosed as suffering from unfortunately left no room for hope. The two sisters visited him every day, so that he should not feel too alone, and Mr Davies was very grateful to them.

Meanwhile the preparations were in full swing for the concert, which was to take place on 15 December. Every evening the girls met for rehearsals and everywhere there was a great bustle and not a little confusion. At last the long awaited day arrived. The concert was a great success; among the various contributions Dorothy's performance was one of the best. It was a revelation to both Gwendolyn and Clare, who had never heard her secretary play. 'What a delicate touch and what a romantic interpretation!' exclaimed Clare. Gwendolyn added, 'A real artist!'

A few days later the students returned to their homes for Christmas. Dorothy preferred to go without the few days of holiday that were due to her, for she could no longer accept the rigid religious intransigence of her father, who belonged to the puritan sect of the Plymouth Brethren.

Gwendolyn took advantage of Dorothy's presence to get to know her better. In fact the girl did not have much to do during the college vacation and knew the area well. So she was able to arrange one or two outings in the neighbourhood, so that Gwendolyn should get to know it too. During these walks the latter told many stories about her life in India; the long journeys around the province with her husband, the social life and the festivities in Calcutta in the Governor of Bengal's palace, the kindness and often the destitution of the Indian people ... Dorothy evinced a lively interest in the lady's stories, which transported her mentally into a world unfamiliar to her. Often on their return from these walks, while they were having a cup of tea with Clare, Gwendolyn would open her photograph albums, which she had brought with her from India. These pictures fired the imagination of Dorothy still further. What with the walks, visits to the hospital and to friends seen again after the long years of separation, the Christmas vacation passed very quickly, and the friendship between Dorothy and Gwendolyn deepened steadily.

Chapter 2

After the Christmas break life at Victoria College resumed its normal course. Clare, Gwendolyn and Dorothy were more and more involved in giving a boost to the students' activities. In this way the winter passed without incident. Even the father's health seemed to have taken a turn for the better, and the sisters began to hope, not so much for a cure, but at least for a stabilization in his condition. The end arrived suddenly. On the afternoon of 16 April, Dr Watson, their private doctor, rang from the hospital to say, 'Come quickly. Your father is very seriously ill'. Clare and Gwendolyn hurried to the hospital, but when they arrived they found their father already in a coma. He had had a stroke, the seriousness of which was only too obvious. The two sisters spent some very painful hours at their father's bedside, until the end came. As dawn was breaking on 17 April, Mr Davies died.

Gwendolyn sent her husband the sad news in a telegram, adding that a long letter would follow. This reached Major Waterhouse at the end of May and began as follows:

'Dear Liam,
 I can't begin to tell you what we felt when our father died. Clare and I were beginning to hope for a miracle, but it was not to be ... and the end came suddenly'.

The letter went on with further details about her father's death and asked if she could stay on a while at Egham, as this would be of great comfort to both Clare and herself. She went on to say that the return journey to Calcutta during the hot weather and the monsoon that would soon be upon them would not be too much to her liking. The letter ended with a good piece of news:

'I think I have found the solution to our problems concerning the upbringing of our grandchildren. I have met here at Victoria College a delightful girl, well educated and available for a change of life, and (for the moment) free of family ties.

She is the private secretary of my sister Clare. I'm toying with the idea of returning to India with her. I haven't yet spoken to her because I first want to hear what you think. But I'm sure you'll trust my judgement. I can assure you that during these months while I've been staying at the college, I've come to have a high opinion of Dorothy's qualities.

Your Gwendolyn.'

The answer from Major Waterhouse was a telegram a month later: 'Expecting you and Dorothy in October. Liam.'

Gwendolyn's offer to Dorothy to go with her to India was at first received with astonishment, which quickly turned to joy and delight. Dorothy told her father about this offer of Gwendolyn's, which she said she would like to accept. He replied gravely that she should think very carefully about it. But Dorothy stood firmly by her decision.

The two days preceding Monday 15 September, which was the day their ship left for India, were spent packing. There was a great deal of luggage, but the friends were not worried about transport, for they knew that both at Egham and in London porters were plentiful. They had also been told that the ship, the SS *Simla*, which they were to travel on, would not weigh anchor at Tilbury before six o'clock in the evening at high tide.

On the morning of the 15th, after a quick early breakfast, Gwendolyn and Dorothy, with Clare's assistance, had their many suitcases loaded on to the college coach and left for Egham station to travel to Waterloo. From there they took a taxi to Tilbury. During these journeys the ladies, overcome with emotion, did not talk very much. Gwendolyn was thinking that in barely a month she would be seeing and embracing her loved ones. Dorothy was sad, thinking of her father and mother, whom perhaps she would not see again and who had said goodbye to her only in a letter of farewell. However she was also letting her imagination run on her future life, rich with possibilities but full of uncertainties. Clare, with this departure, was losing at one and the same time her sister and a valuable friend and helper.

When the taxi drove on to the quayside where the ship for India was moored, it was at once surrounded by a swarm of porters, waiting to

*Chapter 2*

load the luggage on board, and the three ladies had difficulty in alighting amidst an indescribable confusion. Then they went up the gangway ... Clare stayed on the ship with her sister and Dorothy for the final farewells as long as possible, till loud blasts on the ship's siren were heard and members of the crew, running along the decks and the corridors were calling out, 'All non-passengers on shore'. It was a terrible moment. Clare kissed her sister and Dorothy passionately for the last time and then left quickly without turning round so that they should not see her crying. Once on land, she joined the group of friends and relations who were waving handkerchiefs to say goodbye to the SS *Simla* as it left its berth.

# Chapter 3

The assassination of Archduke Ferdinand of Austria at Sarajevo on 28 June 1914 at first aroused little interest in England. The *Times* published only a short paragraph reporting the fact. But towards the end of July rumours of an imminent European war grew ever more insistent. Nevertheless Gwendolyn and Dorothy had decided against altering their arrangements and to leave all the same. When the SS *Simla* set sail from Tilbury, the news coming from the Western Front was bad: the Germans had advanced rapidly into Belgium and France and were threatening to seize Paris. The captain had received an urgent cablegram warning of the possibility of German U-boat attacks. He therefore thought it necessary to call all the passengers together into suitable rooms and to acquaint them with the latest news and tell them of the rules to be observed on board ship. In particular he said, 'During the hours of darkness there must be no lights visible from outside, not even cigarettes. Tomorrow morning we shall begin boat drill on board, and this will be repeated for several days, so that you will be ready for any emergency. I am sure every one of you will collaborate with the crew to maintain good order with British discipline.'

Gwendolyn and Dorothy were tired after their long day and the variety of experiences they had gone through and they went off to their cabin. After a little freshen up they lay down on their bunks for a short rest...

They woke up when the stewardess knocked on their door to tell them that dinner was already on the table. The two ladies dressed quickly and joined the other passengers who had already started their dinner.

The first class dining room was elegantly decorated and contained round tables with six places per table, laid with fine porcelain, crystal glasses and silver cutlery. The chairs were upholstered in red velvet of the same colour and material as the long curtains that covered the portholes. The steward showed Gwendolyn and Dorothy to the table and

# The Queen of The Hills

places assigned to them. There were already four persons sitting at the table: a distinguished looking elderly gentleman, two pretty girls about twenty years old and a dark haired young man of about thirty. With a quick glance Gwendolyn summed up the foursome and muttered to Dorothy, 'Nice company!' The two gentlemen got up and bowed to the ladies, who took their places with a smile.

'Please excuse us for being late', said Dorothy. 'We've had a long day and we went right off to sleep. We shall be punctual in future.'

'We too were worn out,' said Jessica, the younger of the two girls, 'but out appetite got the better of us.'

The elderly doctor, Ian Andrews, intervened, 'Think nothing of it. Your delightful company will be ample compensation for your lateness.'

While everyone was smiling at the doctor's sally, Lilly, the older girl, exclaimed, 'Oh well done, sir. You want to make a conquest.' And they all burst out laughing.

While the ladies were waiting for the first course to be served, they had time to have a closer look at their fellow diners. The two gentlemen were obviously professional men of some sort; one near the end of his career, the other near the beginning. The older man was short and stocky with white hair and a white beard and a moustache, which gave him an air of great dignity and authority. The younger man also had an air of authority, as if he was accustomed to giving orders and being obeyed. He owed this not only to his personality but to the fact that he was above average height and of athletic build with a firm set mouth and jaw. He had eyes that looked straight at you as he spoke, and you were aware that here was a man that was ambitious and would go far.

What did this young man make of the two ladies that arrived late to dinner? The older was a *grande dame* typical of the English upper bourgeoisie, one that had been to a good school and had learnt to obey and be obeyed, especially the latter. It was the younger lady, however, that attracted the young man's interest. She was beautiful in an almost regal way. As she walked, she carried herself very erect; an unconscious mannerism that showed off her long neck to maximum advantage. Her crowning glory was her long golden hair, slightly tinged with red,

## Chapter 3

which the fashion of the time required to be tied up in a bun at the back of her head, thus destroying some of its effect. When she spoke, she did so in a quiet ethereal way that held the hearer's attention. It was a very sweet voice.

The young man, who had not yet spoken, introduced himself, 'My name is Farley Oates, and I'm returning to Calcutta to resume my work as a lecturer in history at the university there.'

Gwendolyn then spoke, 'I too am returning to my family in Calcutta. My husband is Major Liam Waterhouse, advisor to the Governor of Bengal, and my name is Gwendolyn. My friend is Miss Dorothy Ollis, who is keeping me company during the voyage.'

At this moment Dorothy added, 'My dear Gwendolyn, you have left out the most important thing; namely that I'm to be the governess of your grand-children.'

Dinner continued amidst joyful chatter. Towards the end the Purser, Commander Carter, went the round of the tables, introducing himself and enquiring if there were any passengers that would be willing to entertain their fellows in any way: music, recitations, jokes or games. There would be several evenings of festivities organized on board. These would help to dissipate the mood of gloom caused by the war news which had previously been given out. Gwendolyn immediately put forward Dorothy's name, saying, 'My friend, Miss Ollis, is a very good pianist.' Dorothy answered, 'I accept on one condition: that Mr Oates and Dr Andrews keep me company.' Farley said, 'I agree. I've brought along with me some comic poems I've written which may cause some amusement. What do you think?' Lilly then spoke up excitedly, 'I can't wait to hear them.' Jessica offered to sing a song.

The Purser was highly pleased with such a ready response to his proposal and turning to the doctor said, 'I'm sure that you too, Dr Andrews, will be able to make some contribution to the entertainment.'

'I know a few card tricks, but I'm not so sure if ...'

'You're booked,' was the officer's prompt reply, and he added, 'During the next few days you will be invited to attend rehearsals.' He then passed on to the other tables.

# The Queen of The Hills

Dinner was over and everyone congratulated the steward on the excellent cuisine. Jessica and Lilly, who were very tired, took their leave at once and went to their cabin. Dr Andrews, turning to his fellow guests, said, 'What do you say to a turn round the deck? It's a fine night.' The suggestion was taken up and the four went off chatting. The ladies put over their shoulders the shawls they had brought with them and were followed by the gentlemen into the cool night air. They stopped for a while to lean on the rail and admire the lovely night; the clear star-studded sky with a waxing half moon which was reflected in the calm sea. Suddenly the sound of a piano came to their ears. Their curiosity was aroused and they went off in the direction of the sound. They came to a saloon where there were several couples dancing to the sound of a piano: it was the piano bar. The little group sat down at a table, and Dr Andrews ordered a bottle of champagne to make a toast to the happy outcome of the voyage. After the toast they stayed on for a while listening to the music and then retired to their cabins.

About two o'clock in the morning – only an hour or two after the passengers had gone to sleep – the sirens on board began to boom out intermittently, the signal for imminent danger. At the same time members of the crew ran along the ship's corridors ringing a bell and shouting, 'Alarm! Alarm! Everyone to their boat drill stations.' The cabin doors began opening and people in dressing gowns, half-asleep and scared, rushed along the corridors towards the decks.

'What's going on? Why have we been woken up? Is it an exercise?' These were the questions that passengers insistently asked the crew members, without getting any clear answers. Meanwhile the engines of the ship had speeded up their rhythm and the SS *Simla* had changed direction. Dorothy and Gwendolyn, hurrying out of their cabin, found the places previously assigned to them on the deck, in spite of the considerable general confusion that reigned. Suddenly the captain's voice was heard loud and clear, calling for silence on the part of the passengers. 'Ladies and gentlemen, this is not an exercise. A German U-boat has been spotted, but fortunately we have managed to avoid it by changing direction. We shall not be out of danger till we reach Gibraltar. I therefore call upon you all to co-operate and maintain

## Chapter 3

order as much as possible. Boat drill will take place tomorrow morning at ten thirty. Thank you and good night.'

Farley had seen the two ladies in the crowd just as the captain began to speak. When the speech was over, Farley went over to them, trying to allay their fears as they were very agitated. They were then joined by Jessica and Lilly, who were crying and wished they had not taken the decision to join their brother in India at such a dramatic and dangerous time.

'Why oh why,' said Lilly, 'did the Kaiser choose this time to start a war?' Her question raised a smile among those that heard her, while Jessica made a sign to her not to say any more. Then everybody went off to their cabins.

Chapter 4

The next day, notwithstanding the sleepless night, all the passengers were ready at ten thirty to carry out the boat drill already announced. Everything went off as it should, as the previous night's scare had made everyone more attentive. The passengers found their places as quickly as possible; they donned their life jackets and identified the lifeboats they should go to in case of danger. The captain's voice was heard: 'Ladies and gentlemen, last night there was considerable chaos, understandable in view of your fear and the unexpected alarm. This morning, as you will be aware, things went much better. The next boat drill, the time of which will not be announced beforehand, will, I am sure, go off perfectly. Now enjoy yourselves and leave the worries to us.' The passengers, who now at last felt relieved of their anxieties, clapped the captain loudly and dispersed in various directions.

Farley invited Gwendolyn and Dorothy to play bowls on the deck as the weather was fine. Gwendolyn excused herself and said she would rather sit in the sun on a deck chair and have a rest, as she was rather tired. Dorothy said, 'I accept, but you'll have to be patient with me because I don't know how to play.' While they were on their way, a steward came up and asked, 'Are you Miss Ollis? You're invited this evening after dinner to perform in the rehearsals that will be held in the Assembly Room in preparation for the gala next Saturday.' Dorothy said she would be there but was rather overawed.

'And I was hoping to invite you to dance this evening,' said Farley.

Dorothy replied, 'Unfortunately I don't dance very well. The unbending religious principles of my father always prevented me from indulging in any amusement, however innocent, which he considered worldly. Dancing was one of these. To be honest, I no longer hold his very narrow religious beliefs, which have made me very unhappy. I may add that this was one of the reasons that prompted me into accepting Mrs Waterhouse's offer and leaving England, perhaps for many years.'

# The Queen of The Hills

'I'm now beginning to understand you a bit better,' replied Farley. 'But let's banish sad thoughts and go and play bowls.' He took her by the hand and they went on deck.

Dorothy spent an hour or two playing with Farley in the open air. He taught her the game. But during lunchtime the weather changed. Big waves, topped with white horses, rocked the ship. Many passengers hurried over their lunches and retired to their cabins to ward off seasickness.

Gwendolyn and Dorothy went to the reading room, as previously arranged, to write some letters, which would be posted on their arrival at Malta. One of these was for Clare, and in it they told her all about the voyage so far. Then Gwendolyn wrote to her husband to allay any fears he might have on reading disturbing newspaper reports about U-boats. The ship had in fact changed course and was making a wider circle to avoid attacks, if possible. Dorothy prepared a letter in the same vein for her parents, as she did not want them to worry about her.

While the ladies were writing, an unusually big wave struck the ship. Many passengers, seized with panic, left their cabins shouting and afraid that a torpedo had hit them. The voice of the captain was then heard, 'We are going through a squall, but the worst is now over. In a few hours we shall reach calm water. I urge everyone to remain calm.' The two friends, who like everyone else had had a big fright, were reassured and resumed their writing.

That evening at dinner the main talking point of all the diners was of course the squall, fortunately now over, and the scare they had had. At our friends' table Jessica and Lilly were missing. Dr Andrews asked a steward to enquire the reason for their absence. The answer came straight-away, 'They're not feeling well.'

After dinner the four of them made their way to the Assembly Room where the rehearsals for the gala were due to be held. When they got there the doctor left the group saying, 'Excuse me for leaving you, but I'm on the organizing committee that has been given the job by the Purser of arranging the social activities on board.' Indeed at that moment Commander Carter came into the room and told those that were present of the creation of the organizing committee, whose job it

## Chapter 4

would be to choose those that were to take part in the gala evenings. About a dozen people performed one after the other. One of the earliest to do so was Dorothy, who played a Chopin mazurka. Her performance was so outstanding that everyone clapped loudly. As soon as she had finished, Farley went up to her and, helping her down from the platform, gallantly kissed her hand.

'You're a great pianist! I think that in comparison all the other performers will seem second rate amateurs, including me of course.'

Dorothy, quite overcome, more because her hand was kissed than because of the compliments she received, went with Farley to a settee to listen to the other performances. While Lilly was preparing to sing her song *Daisy*, Farley whispered to Dorothy, 'My contribution has been put off till a later evening. So, my dear Miss Ollis, I shall be able to listen to you calmly on Saturday. Later on I would like to have your advice in choosing the poem I should read.'

'I should love to,' replied Dorothy. 'But now let's listen to Lilly.'

Lilly's little song went off so nicely that everyone joined in the chorus. The last person to perform was Dr Andrews, who left his seat on the panel of judges to become an actor. He did some card tricks with such skill that he left all those present quite bewildered. They gave him a warm round of applause. He advanced to the edge of the platform and said, 'I'm lucky. I've found another job to keep me busy when I retire.' And the audience burst into loud laughter.

Chapter 5

The ship proceeded on its way; the evening and night passed without incident. The next morning all our friends were at the table punctually for breakfast. The rehearsals of the previous evening were naturally the chief topic of conversation. Gwendolyn and Jessica, who had not been present at the rehearsals, were curious to know what had happened.

'Wait till tomorrow. You will see,' exclaimed Dr Andrews with a smile of connivance at Dorothy. As soon as Jessica and Lilly had finished their breakfast, they announced that they had to leave the table at once, because two nice young men, whom they pointed out sitting at the table at some distance from theirs, were waiting to take them for a stroll round the deck. 'Here they are, coming over,' said the girls with a delicate blush.

'How delightful,' said Gwendolyn. 'You mustn't keep them waiting.' Meanwhile Dr Andrews also excused himself. Then Farley, turning to the two ladies, said, 'May I ask you too, Mrs Waterhouse, to listen while I read some of my comic poems to help me choose the most suitable to read in public. I've got them with me.'

The ladies agreed, but they first wanted to take a turn round the deck for a bit of fresh air. It was a lovely morning and the warm sun invited the passengers into the open air. The ship was approaching Gibraltar and the change of latitude could be felt.

At about half past ten the organizing committee met in the Assembly Room to settle the final details of the gala the following evening. Meanwhile Farley and the two ladies finished their walk and found a quiet sunny spot on the deck chairs. When they were settled, Farley took a little black book out of his pocket and began to read a poem.

Suddenly the dismal sound of the ship's siren was heard. Farley broke off in the middle of a sentence, taken aback, and all three cried out simultaneously, 'The alarm!' They got up quickly and made their way to their assembly points. When everyone was in position, the captain spoke, 'This is an exercise and it had gone off very well. Unfortunately we have just received the news that a passenger ship, the SS *London*, *en route* for England, has been attacked and hit by a U-boat. There is no further information, but this stresses the importance of these boat drills.'

After the captain's speech, the passengers resumed their previous activities so as to avoid revealing their worries. The ladies discussed the dresses they would wear the following evening. The gentlemen laid bets on which lady would be honoured with an invitation to the captain's table. Many names were put forward, not least Dorothy's. The 'actors' selected to entertain at the gala were very worried about the success of their performance. Farley, whose reading had been interrupted by the alarm, again asked Gwendolyn and Dorothy to advise him on the choice of a poem to be read. From the ones that he read the ladies chose *The Story of Aden*, which they considered the most amusing, especially as it was read in a very comic accent.

At dinnertime Lilly arrived at the table in a state of agitation: she had not yet found anyone capable of accompanying her on the piano during her song. She gave Dorothy an imploring look and asked her, 'Couldn't you play for me, Miss Ollis? You play so well.' Dorothy smiled and replied, 'Come, come! Don't look so worried. If there is really no one else to play for you, I will gladly do so, provided you've got the music.' Lilly, all smiles again, exclaimed, 'Yes, there's the music, I've been assured, and with your support *Daisy* will be a great success.' Dr Andrews then spoke, 'My dear Lilly, *Daisy* was a great success yesterday. What more do you want?' Jessica replied, 'I can't wait for tomorrow to be over, because now my sister is quite impossible.'

Immediately after lunch Gwendolyn and Dorothy took leave of their fellow diners to go to their cabin. Dorothy in particular wanted to think about the events of the last few days and the fact that Farley had so quickly taken a liking to her, a liking that she returned. She was almost inclined to reveal her feelings to Gwendolyn, but that seemed to her somewhat premature in view of the turmoil she felt inside herself. However Gwendolyn had already sensed quite a lot, even if she did not show it openly, as the situation was a little delicate.

Chapter 6

For dinner on Saturday evening the first class dining room was decorated with particular splendour. When Jessica and Lilly reached their table, they were surprised to see that it had only been laid for four and asked the steward for an explanation. He said, 'Mrs Waterhouse and Dr Andrews have been invited this evening to dine at the captain's table.'

'Just those two?' said Lilly, a little put out.

The steward comforted her saying, 'Your turn will come one day, rest assured.'

The entrance of Gwendolyn and Dorothy, particularly elegant in their evening dresses, made many heads turn and look at them. While the first was making her way to the captain's table, the second sat down with Lilly and Jessica. 'You look lovely this evening, Miss Ollis,' exclaimed Lilly. Dorothy smiled pleasantly and thanked her for the compliment, while she cast her mind back gratefully to the dressmaker at Victoria College who had helped her to make up that model.

The last to arrive at dinner was Farley, who was quite taken aback, seeing the three ladies even more bewitching than usual. Dorothy turned to him and said, 'Sit down, Mr Oates; we're waiting for you. This evening out friends have deserted us for the delights of the captain's table. We were feeling quite alone.'

Farley reparteed smartly, 'I don't think you would have remained so for long.' This display of gallantry made the girls giggle.

The dinner was excellent, and the wines that were served were much appreciated. All the diners were in a good humour as they moved to the Assembly Room and were ready to enjoy the gala evening. They were looking forward to the beginning of the show, so they were all rather disappointed when they saw the captain mount the platform, for he seemed intent on making another speech. The passengers had had enough of these during the previous days, but out of courtesy to him they resigned themselves to listening to what he had to say, hoping that he would not drag it out too long.

He began, 'Ladies and gentlemen, before the show begins, I think you would be pleased to know that during dinner we arrived in sight of Gibraltar. Right now we are passing through the straits, so I'm sure you will not want to miss the chance of seeing the rock, even at a distance, and even if that slightly delays the start of the show. Shall we say – back here in half an hour?'

A burst of applause and hurrahs greeted this announcement. Everyone spontaneously broke into *Land of Hope and Glory*.

At this point some explanation is due to account for this sudden change in the behaviour of the passengers, which could cause surprise. It must be remembered that the war had been raging for barely six weeks; a war that all the combatants had entered into with tremendous enthusiasm, certain that they would come out of it the victors before Christmas. Everyone on board the SS *Simla* had been living in a state of tension for almost a week because of the U-boat threat. Now the passage of the straits of Gibraltar removed this danger. For in the eyes of the English of that period, was not the Mediterranean their *Mare nostrum*? Furthermore Gibraltar itself made the breasts of those same English swell with patriotic pride. In addition Cape Trafalgar was not far off, where the British Navy had won a battle, whose date every English schoolboy knows.

As for *Land of Hope and Glory*, the dreadfully chauvinistic words had been written recently to be sung to a splendid tune written twenty years previously by Edward Elgar. Elgar himself disapproved of the words, and rightly so, but that did not prevent the song becoming an immediate success in England, as it perfectly expressed the feelings of the English of that period.

When the passengers of the SS *Simla* had finished singing with the utmost fervour they were capable of, they poured out on to the decks to gaze at the massive rock, which lost none of its splendour, though the night was coming on. They stayed there filled with admiration for the thirty minutes suggested by the captain. Then they went back into the Assembly Room, patriotically uplifted and more than ever impatient for the show to begin. It did so immediately.

Dr Andrews had been given the job of introducing the various people that were to perform. The items followed one after the other.

## Chapter 6

Then he announced the last one: 'Now, here is what you have all been waiting for: Miss Dorothy Ollis will perform a mazurka of Chopin.'

From the very first note, the audience realized that they were listening to a great pianist. The silence was total and the mazurka rang out crisply in the air. At the end of the piece there was still a moment of silence, and then everyone rose from his seat and clapped furiously shouting 'Encore!' Dorothy, though somewhat overwhelmed by this enthusiastic reaction, bowed and then nodded her head. In a firm voice she said, 'I will play the great polonaise by Chopin.' Again the magic of the music swept over the audience. At the end there was a real ovation.

Farley, seeing that Dorothy was overcome and tired after her performance, made his way through the crowd to the platform and helped her down. Together they went over to Gwendolyn. Meanwhile the Purser announced that the festivities would continue with dancing for those that wished. Gwendolyn and Farley congratulated Dorothy warmly on the pleasure they had derived from Chopin's lovely music.

Gwendolyn said, 'At the college I had already come to the conclusion that you were a good pianist, but until this evening I had not had occasion to appreciate your talents to the full. I hope that you will be able to teach my grandson Alan to play as well.'

Dorothy replied, 'That will give me great pleasure. And now, if you will excuse me, I must go to my cabin because I'm very tired.'

Chapter 7

The next day was Sunday, and a religious service had been fixed for eleven o'clock on the main deck. Many passengers attended it and among these were our friends: Dorothy and Gwendolyn, Farley and Dr Andrews. Lilly and Jessica, on the other hand, preferred to walk on deck with their young men.

Before the service the captain inspected the crew in the presence of the passengers to ensure that everything was ship-shape. At the inspection the Lascars, dressed in white with red turbans and belts, made a brave show. The cooks in their white uniforms were also very smart; they paraded between the Lascars and the British sailors, dressed in blue.

The service, read by the captain, was regarded as a moment of spiritual uplift after the days of fear in the Atlantic and also as a plea for help for all those directly involved in the war. The hymns too, chosen for the occasion, reflected the mood of the passengers, so much so that they were hardly aware of the hardness of the deck they were kneeling on, which was particularly noticeable when the ship rolled.

The passengers spent the rest of that day and the following days until they arrived at Malta, the first port of call, as pleasantly as possible. The committee organized games, competitions and various kinds of activities, and the young people above all joined in with gusto.

It was announced that the ship would reach Malta between 1800 and 1900 hours on Wednesday, and everyone was looking forward to landing after being cooped up on board for nine long days. They were eager to visit the city of Valletta, go shopping, but especially to send off their mail and hear the latest news on the present situation in Europe.

On Wednesday afternoon Gozo was sighted, a parched rocky island with few inhabitants. Two hours later Malta was seen, and someone who was familiar with the island pointed out the statue of St Paul overlooking the bay where he was shipwrecked. Without difficulty the ship sailed into the Quarantine harbour. The entrance was really impressive. The sun had set and in the distance one could see the quayside and the city with their lights twinkling. The passengers, excited by the arrival, lined the rail of the main deck to enjoy the sight. Shortly afterwards they saw a launch heave to, with the medical inspector on board to carry out the routine inspection and checks. When these had been completed, other people could come on board. One of the first of these was a gentleman accompanied by the Purser, who introduced him to Gwendolyn.

'My name is Marco Pizzini,' said the Maltese gentleman. 'I learnt of your arrival, Mrs Waterhouse, from a telegram sent me by your husband, an old comrade in arms of mine. I also have here a letter of introduction for you.' Whereupon he offered to show Gwendolyn round the city on the following day. She was surprised and pleased at the unexpected visit and answered, 'That is very kind of you, Mr Pizzini. Would it be possible to bring my friends along?'

'By all means, so long as there are no more than ten of them. I shall call for you on the stroke of nine and will show you Valletta.' Then Mr Pizzini took his leave.

That evening at dinner Gwendolyn gave her friends the good news.

'Tomorrow morning a dear friend of long standing of my husband is coming to pick us up in his boat. So we must all be ready at nine. You too, Jessica and Lilly with your nice young men. We shall all have a guided tour of Valletta.'

The reaction was noisy and joyful, but Lilly was worried and asked, 'Shall we have to walk a lot?'

'No,' replied Gwendolyn, 'We shall go in carriages.'

Farley, squeezing Dorothy's hand, muttered, 'Tomorrow we shall have the whole day together.' And Dorothy squeezed back.

The next day breakfast was served very early, and everyone hurried to the dining room so as to be ready for the arrival of the boats to take them on shore. The Purser had in fact announced that the SS *Simla* would set sail at 2200 hours, and so the passengers had the whole day free to spend on shore. While they were waiting happily for this moment, a mail bag was delivered with letters and parcels for passengers and crew, and the Purser arranged for the rapid distribution of these so

## Chapter 7

as not to delay the disembarkation. At once they all started to read their correspondence. While Farley was reading the letter he had received from his family, his face suddenly darkened, and Dorothy noticed.

'What is it?' she asked, 'Bad news?'

'My brother, like so many others of our countrymen, has joined up and will shortly be sent to France. I'm naturally very worried about him.'

Punctually at nine Gwendolyn saw Mr Pizzini's boat arrive. Turning to her friends she said, 'Everyone ready to go ashore? Let's go. They're waiting for us.'

Lilly and Jessica arrived at that moment with their young men. They introduced them, and then the whole group descended to Mr Pizzini's boat. Gwendolyn introduced them one by one. When it was Farley's turn, he said, 'I'm very glad to meet you, Mr Pizzini. I teach history at the University of Calcutta, and I hope that you will be able to give me some detailed information about the history of Malta.'

Mr Pizzini replied in embarrassment. 'You, sir, probably know more about it than I do.'

Lilly said, 'I would prefer to go to a nice restaurant for a special lunch.' All the others, more than anything else, wanted to visit the city. Mr Pizzini smiled and answered diplomatically, 'There will be time for everything. Today in Valletta there is a big fiesta to celebrate the defeat of the Turks in 1565, and this evening at nine there will also be a firework display.'

Chatting and laughing, they tied up at the quayside, where they disembarked. Here two carriages were waiting for them. In the first there were seats for Gwendolyn, Dorothy, Farley, Dr Andrews and of course for Mr Pizzini who was the guide. Lilly and Jessica got into the second with their young men. Mr Pizzini gave a nod to the coachmen and off they went. The party was surprised to hear the babble of voices, many of which were speaking a mixture of Arabic, Italian and Maltese. Street traders were offering goods of various sorts. But the carriages went on till they reached St George's Square, and there they stopped. The group alighted to admire the square and in particular to read what was written in large letters in Latin on the building called 'Main Guard':

## MAGNAE ET INVICTAE BRITANNIAE AMOR MELITENSIUM ET VOX EUROPAE HAS INSULAS CONFIRMANT. AD 1814

Dorothy turning to Farley said to him in jest, 'Professor, you know Latin. Please translate for us what is written there.'

'Certainly, but the lesson ends here. The inscription says, "The love of the Maltese and the voice of Europe grant these islands to Great Britain the invincible".'

There was a moment of embarrassed silence. Pizzini, ever the diplomat, added, 'Look carefully at the date.'

Then the group got into their carriages again and continued their tour. They went towards the city centre, where the group stopped again to admire the Opera House and to visit the cathedral, St John's, where they stayed for some time. When they came out, Lilly said she was a little tired and would like to go and have lunch. The other ladies agreed with her. Dr Andrews and Farley invited Mr Pizzini to have lunch with them and asked him to suggest a good restaurant. He recommended the Hyde Park Corner Restaurant. This name aroused general hilarity in the group. Only Mr Pizzini could not enjoy the joke and was a little bewildered.

'There's a nice name to remind us of London and a pretty part of the city,' said Dorothy. 'Let's go there.'

The lunch was excellent and everyone was pleased with the Maltese cuisine. Near the end of the meal, Dr Andrews, who guessed that the young people would like to be alone, suggested that the party should split up so that each person should go his own way and spend the rest of the day as he chose, saying, 'Let's meet back at the ship to have dinner and to watch the fireworks afterwards.'

'Mrs Waterhouse,' said Farley, 'may I steal the company of Dorothy for a few hours? I promise you we shall be back punctually for dinner.'

Dorothy blushed at these words and Gwendolyn smiled, 'I have complete confidence in you.'

# Chapter 8

Farley hailed a carriage and got in with Dorothy. They set off for the Great Harbour. Once there they admired the splendour of it, which made it one of the finest in the world. They continued on their tour leaving the itinerary to be chosen by the driver, who pointed out to them, as they drove, the streets, buildings and anything worthy of note. The little tour ended back in St George's Square, where they left the carriage and went to a little café with the inviting name of 'Speranza' with many tables outside where they could listen to the band that was giving a concert in the square. Many other people had had the same idea, so the café tables were almost all full. The gay tuneful music rounded off in the best possible way the pleasant afternoon that the two young people had spent together. But they had arrived a little too late, as the concert came to an end shortly afterwards and many people left.

'Now at least we can talk,' said Farley. 'I have been waiting for this moment, as we have so many things to talk about. May I call you Dorothy?'

'Certainly, Farley. Tell me a little about yourself and your life in India.'

'Well, India has always attracted me. You see, it offers a young man so many chances of getting on in the world and so bettering himself, much more than England does. This is my second voyage out after a six months holiday at home. I wanted to join up like my brother at this moment in our history, but the Ministry for the Colonies told me that my presence would be more useful in India. Tell me, why do you want to go to India? You have already told me about the severity of your father, but you haven't explained to me quite why you made this decision, nor how you came to know Mrs Waterhouse.'

Dorothy told him about the events of the previous winter and added, 'I accepted Gwendolyn's offer with joy and trepidation. Joy because I shall be living in a new and interesting environment, and trepidation because I don't know what is in store for me.'

At these words Farley smiled, and looking her straight in the eyes, whispered, 'Fate may already have decided on something for you.' Then he took her hand and kissed it. Dorothy neither turned away from his gaze nor withdrew her hand from the kiss. Just at that moment the clock in the square struck six.

'Oh,' exclaimed Dorothy coming back to reality. 'It's getting late. We promised to be back on board for dinner.'

'Don't worry, we've got plenty of time to be there before seven.'

The party was all back punctually for dinner: Lilly and Jessica, Dorothy and Farley, Gwendolyn, Dr Andrews and Mr Pizzini, who had been pressed into staying for dinner too. Everyone wanted to tell of their adventures, and the conversation buzzed backwards and forwards. The girls were in the seventh heaven of delight because they had been invited by their young men to join them in watching the fireworks and in going to the dance that had been arranged for afterwards on board.

Later, while they were finishing their meal, the first explosions were heard, and the passengers poured out onto the deck, an excellent position for watching the display. A brilliant variety of colour and shapes was reflected in the water. There were shouts of amazement, one after the other, as the harbour and city were seen splendidly lit up. About ten o'clock, while the passengers were still engrossed in the spectacle, a familiar voice was heard on the loudspeaker, 'All non-passengers on shore.' This was a brutal return to reality. Farley, taking advantage of the general confusion, put his arm round the bare shoulders of Dorothy and drew her gently towards himself. This action did not escape Gwendolyn's notice. Mr Pizzini, who had spent the day agreeably with his guests, shook their hands warmly. They thanked him for his kindness, and he then left the ship. During the explosion of the last few fireworks, the ship's engines changed rhythm and the ship set sail into the darkness of the night and to the open sea.

## Chapter 9

Next morning the change of climate was noticeable. It was warmer and also the sailors were wearing their white tropical uniforms. The passengers had before them three days of sailing on the high seas. The committee already referred to, therefore, got busy organizing games during the day to avoid boredom and in the evening dancing and variety shows. The games were quoits, croquet and ping-pong, both singles and doubles. The latter could either be previously arranged or drawn by lot. Farley and Dorothy at once put their names down as partners for quoits. Both of them were good at games and they quickly became the favourite pair and won many fans. Dr Andrews and Gwendolyn were partners in croquet.

That evening the sun lit up the western sky with brilliant splashes of colour like a kaleidoscope. Many passengers stayed on deck to admire the spectacle. A sailor that was passing by took all the romance out of the show by saying, 'There'll be a lovely storm tonight.'

In fact at about four o'clock in the morning a very violent one broke. The rain fell so fast that it seemed like an impenetrable wall. The lightning zigzagged incessantly and the thunder made a deafening noise. The wind raised formidable waves and battered the ship violently from stem to stern. The rain went on for two solid hours, and someone on board calculated that there had been more than four inches of rain. Morning arrived with a brilliant sun and a cool breeze. At breakfast the sole subject of conversation was naturally the storm which was barely over, and many passengers admitted to having felt afraid when a particularly violent wave struck. Never before had they had such an experience. Dr Andrews said to the moaners that the storm was merely a foretaste of the monsoon they would experience in India.

During the days that remained before the arrival of the ship at Port Said, the mornings were spent in competitive games and the afternoons in the passengers' private pursuits. The afternoon of the last day in the Mediterranean saw Dorothy and Gwendolyn preparing for the arrival

# The Queen of The Hills

at Port Said: letters to send off and summer clothes to get out for the rest of the voyage. When these duties had been accomplished, the two ladies went up on deck and found two deck chairs to relax on and enjoy the cool air. Gwendolyn was the first to speak and asked, 'Dorothy, we haven't had much time for a private conversation these last few days. I now want to ask you a personal question. What do you think of Mr Oates?'

Dorothy answered, 'I know what's on your mind, and I wanted to speak to you about it myself. Farley's a very nice man, intelligent and cultured. I won't conceal from you that I am fond of him, but I haven't forgotten the obligation I entered upon with you and your family for at least a year, and I shall keep my promise.'

'It's my impression that he's fonder of you than you are of him.'

Dorothy replied to this remark with an enigmatic smile.

The SS *Simla* arrived at Port Said in the course of the night. The passengers were awakened early by the din that was coming from the wharf. Further sleep was impossible, so many people got up to go an see what was happening. The noise was caused by a horde of coolies, black from head to foot, who were carrying coal on to the ship. The heat, the confusion and the clouds of coal dust were such as to drive many people off the ship before breakfast. Dr Andrews and Farley hired a boat and invited Gwendolyn and Dorothy to join them. They were all wearing light clothes as the temperature was quite high. Their first purchase was a hat called topee to protect them from the sun in the Red Sea. Dorothy laughed, 'Farley looks just like a general.' This quip put everyone in a good humour, notwithstanding the fact that they had got up very early and had not breakfasted.

Their stroll through the town was impeded by a throng of street traders and beggars that crowded round them crying out in every language and offering an astonishing variety of goods for sale; among them pornographic postcards, which provoked Farley's ire. The ladies were shocked and were almost inclined to return to the ship straightaway. But to go back was just as difficult as to go forward. In the end there arrived some policemen, in white uniforms and wearing fezzes, who cleared the street somewhat vigorously, allowing the group to walk more freely.

## Chapter 9

On the way they stopped to make some more purchases, and Gwendolyn showed her skill in bargaining, acquired by years of experience in India. Once she had decided on a price, neither the pleas nor the laments of the trader would make her budge.

'Five shillings, lady.'

'I'll give you one, and a half of that will be your profit.'

'Ah, lady how can I live? I make no profit.'

'Rubbish! Do it up.'

And with this the dialogue ended. An Egyptian that witnessed the scene exclaimed in good English, 'By Jove, isn't she hot stuff!'

As they continued walking, the four of them talked about the incident. Farley commented severely, 'What a lot of time is wasted bargaining. I wonder when Orientals will realize that fixed prices in the long run are more profitable.'

But Gwendolyn retorted, 'No, Mr Oates. For them bargaining is a game, a pastime, to which we westerners must adapt ourselves.'

After wandering around the town for an hour and a half, they returned to the harbour. When they were on the quayside where the SS *Simla* was moored, Dorothy noticed the name of the ship and asked, 'Can anyone tell me what SS means?' Dr Andrews explained, 'It means Steam Ship.'

They then returned on board, just in time for breakfast, which they ate with great appetite. They had had enough of Port Said, in spite of its oriental atmosphere and its original picturesque shops. Farley even said that he could never live in Port Said. Obviously he had been greatly upset by the incident on shore. Meanwhile the mailbag and newspapers had been brought on board. Gwendolyn received two long letters: one from her husband and the other from her sister Clare. Dorothy too received a long letter from Clare, in which she said how much she missed her companionship and assistance in the college. The students too remembered her with affection. A short letter from her father gave her family news and urged her to come back to England if the arrangements in Calcutta were not to her taste. Farley was very disappointed not to receive any letters and therefore had to be satisfied with reading the paper. The news was by no means good. The only consolation, if it could be called such, was that the German advance in France had been halted and the front stabilized on the river Aisne. The war would certainly not be over by Christmas, as many people had predicted. Farley thought of his brother and the many other friends who like him had joined up.

The ship left Port Said in the late morning. The passengers crowded the deck to enjoy the spectacle, although it was already very hot. The ship immediately entered the Suez Canal and the speed was reduced to walking pace so that the wash should not damage the banks. On the right of the Canal a railway ran parallel to a strip of greenery consisting of plants and bushes. On the left, however, the countryside was arid. Parched and burnt by the sun; there was not sign of life, not even the possibility of any. The heat on board was such that social life was reduced to a minimum. The *Simla* required the rest of that day and the following night to reach the other end of the Canal. Every time it met another ship, it had to pull into the side and stop. On one of these occasions, a troop ship passed taking Australians and New Zealanders to France. When it was opposite the *Simla* the soldiers that were on deck threw their topees into the water. Dorothy was bewildered by this behaviour and called out, 'Farley, Farley, look. What's going on? What are they doing?'

Farley smiled and answered, 'It's all right. They've not gone mad. They're following the tradition, according to which topees are no use after Suez.' The soldiers were now very near, and several of them, seeing a British ship, called out in jest, 'You're going the wrong way, you're going the wrong way!'

Farley, on hearing these words, muttered bitterly, 'They may be right. I should be going with them.'

The *Simla* reached Suez early the next morning and stopped just long enough to drop the Canal pilot off. It set off at once for the Gulf of Suez and resumed its normal speed. The temperature went up and up, becoming intolerable. In the cabins it started at 95 degrees, gradually reaching 120 or more. The passengers' activities, already reduced, were finally limited to the absolutely indispensable. This uncomfortable state of affairs was expected to last for the five days of the passage of the Red Sea. However the committee, in an effort to raise drooping spirits, organized a brief show. Farley took part in it, reading one of his comic poems. The laughter that this aroused made the passengers forget momentarily the discomfort caused by the heat. At the end of the show, many people preferred not to retire to their cabin to sleep but had their beds brought up on deck; not only men but also a few ladies. This practice was repeated for the five nights that preceded the arrival at Aden.

The days spent in the Red Sea were described by all as hellish, because not even the light breeze that was following the ship brought any relief to the exhausted passengers. The fourth day, when the temperature peaked, there were two dramatic developments. A Lascar, working in the engine room, suffered a stroke and died. Shortly afterwards a second class passenger died from sunstroke. The captain invited everyone to attend the funeral ceremony, which would take place at sundown, of burial at sea of the two unfortunate persons. The ceremony was simple and moving. The two bodies, enveloped in British flags, were slid into the sea in the presence of the crew on parade and the passengers, who were much upset. The chief topic of conversation during that day and the next was, 'Who's next?' The only relief was provided by the fact that Aden was getting near. They reached it at night without further incident after five days out from Suez.

Chapter 10

The ship stayed at Aden the whole night, long enough to load and unload cargo and to re-coal for the next long stretch to Colombo. Nearly all the passengers, exhausted and hoping for a chance to sleep, preferred to stay on board. Only a few men, among them Farley and Dr Andrews, in a spirit of adventure, went on shore to visit the town in spite of the late hour. They strolled along the main street, the only one that was lighted, for a couple of hours. The shops and cafés were all shut, there was nothing of interest to see, and so they went back to the ship, tired and rather disappointed. However those that had stayed on the ship in the hope of sleep were even more disappointed. The din made by the cranes loading the cargo, the chanting of the coolies bringing the coal on board, the black dust that got into everything and forced the passengers to close the portholes and doors in spite of the great heat, made sleep impossible for all but a few.

Farley and Dr Andrews preferred to give up any idea of sleep and went to the saloon to talk while they waited for the *Simla* to set sail. Shortly before the departure, in the half-light of the dawn, they went up on deck for a little cool air. From there they witnessed a most unpleasant scene. An Arab fisherman had come up in his boat to the hull of the *Simla* to sell fish to a steward. The sale had hardly been concluded when the *Simla* started slowly to move. The wash caused the boat to overturn and the Arab was thrown into the sea. In spite of the frantic shouts of the poor fellow and the danger from sharks that infest those waters, the ship continued on its way without anyone trying to help him. Fortunately other fishing folk who had seen his plight left the quay quickly in their boats and rescued him.

Farley and Dr Andrews went off to sleep for an hour or two after the departure. They got up in time for breakfast, which was served about ten, because the passengers had spent an almost sleepless night. No sooner had Farley reached the breakfast table then Dorothy asked him, 'How was your evening in Aden? I very much regretted not joining you, but the heat had deprived me of all energy and the desire to move.'

Farley replied to her, 'My dear, you didn't miss much. Aden is one of our colonies, a Godforsaken rock, where there live, according to my information, two thousand European men, almost all soldiers, a mere three white women and thirty thousand natives. Really I saw very little of the town. Instead, I would like to tell you what Dr Andrews and I saw this morning at dawn as the ship was leaving.' And he recounted what had happened to the unfortunate fisherman.

Gwendolyn, who had listened attentively to the story, was horrified and exclaimed, 'My husband is right when he says that in the East life is worthless.'

The rest of the voyage, which would last another twelve days with a single stop at Colombo, was rather monotonous and without noteworthy incidents. The sole ambition of the passengers was to spend the time in the best possible way, without getting too bored and without consuming too much energy. The hellish temperature in the Red Sea was succeeded by one more moderate. But the increased humidity made life just as uncomfortable. In the relatively cooler hours of the morning and evening, the passengers, at least the younger ones, indulged in some kind of sport, not too energetic, or in strolling round the deck. In the heat of the day, however, everyone tried to find a place to read, write or talk in away from the muggy heat. The saloons with their large fans, which were in continuous operation, or the decks exposed to the wind and out of the sun were among the most popular places. This leisurely atmosphere encouraged the growth of friendship and flirtations. It was a well known fact that many girls from the well off middle class were in the habit at this time of year of joining relatives in India to spend the winter there, enjoying the vigorous social life and hoping to make a good match. A light-hearted name had even been given to the ships carrying these hopefuls – the Fishing Fleet. Those that failed to find a fiancé would return to England the following March and were called – with a lack of gallantry – Returned Empties. Probably Lilly and Jessica did not know these terms, but there was no doubt that they also were part of the Fishing Fleet. At any rate their flirtations went forward swimmingly, and the two girls seemed highly satisfied.

## Chapter 10

The feeling that Farley and Dorothy had for each other, however, was not in the same category and would not end with the arrival in Calcutta. They took advantage of every chance offered by circumstances to get to know each other better, and enjoyed each other's company. So for the two the time passed quickly, while all the other passengers found the voyage to Colombo very long and tedious, in spite of the activities arranged to keep them amused.

The competitions were brought to an end by the arrival at Colombo at one o'clock in the afternoon after six days out from Aden. The stop over at Colombo was due to last for twenty-four hours, so the passengers decided to go ashore in the afternoon. While they were having lunch, a small dark-skinned Singhalese walked smartly through the dining saloon calling out, 'I'm Cook's man'. Farley commented with a laugh, addressing his fellow diners, 'Oh! the universality of Thomas Cook. I wonder if in the whole world there is anywhere that doesn't have a Thomas Cook representative. I really believe that if one day man ever lands on the moon, as soon as he disembarks, he will be accosted by a little green man in a peaked cap, who will say, "Thomas Cook, sir, at your service."' Dorothy immediately added, 'And not far from him, for good measure, there will be a hoarding and written on it will be the words LIPTON'S TEA.'

As the passengers, one by one, finished their lunch, they went aboard P & O Company launches that took them on shore, where it was hotter than on the ship. On the quay dozens and dozens of rickshaws were lined up, in wait for the tourists. For our democratic friends it was a regular shock to see a man treated as a beast of burden. But it was Dorothy who was most upset, seeing a rickshaw for the first time. Sensing her embarrassment the rickshawman said to her with a kind smile, 'Get in, lady, you will like the ride.' Farley handed her in, and they set off, followed by Gwendolyn and Dr Andrews in another rickshaw.

Farley said to the man, 'Take us on a nice tour of the city.' On the way they realized that their man was not only a good driver but also an excellent guide. The four friends were taken to see the most interesting sites in the city: the Hindu and Buddhist temples and the great mosque. Then they arrived at the botanical gardens, where they stopped for a little to admire the magnificent plants. They set off again and passed close to a lake and a field where two teams of Englishmen were playing cricket; they seemed to be back in England. The trip continued with a drive through the city centre, where in the heavy afternoon traffic they had the chance to admire, not only the smart shops, but also the skill of the two rickshawmen in weaving through the general confusion. The next goal was the harbour with the Grand Oriental Hotel for tea. To get there they had to go through the local bazaar with its sordid little shops. Suddenly the rickshawmen stopped in front of one of these, and the first of them bought a single match, with which he lit the lamps of both rickshaws, for fear of being stopped by the police. Soon afterwards they reached the hotel, a large airy building, surrounded by a garden full of flowers and a park, and Farley and Dr Andrews paid the two rickshawmen, adding a fat tip for having been such good guides. So they departed very satisfied.

The two couples of friends went into the tearoom and sat down at a table. The room was very elegant and the air cooled by large fans constantly rotating. There was also a good orchestra that was performing Viennese waltzes. In short, highly desirable surroundings. A few couples were dancing, and so after their tea Farley invited Dorothy to dance. While the couple were going off, Dr Andrews who had got up saw sitting at a table not too far off Dr Ballantyne, a colleague of his in the Indian medical service. There was great mutual surprise at meeting each other in Colombo, and at the same time delight at seeing each other again. Dr Ballantyne invited his friends and Mrs Waterhouse to his table. After the introductions he exclaimed, 'What are you doing here, Ian, so far from Darjeeling?'

'I've been spending six months on holiday at home in Scotland,' was the answer. 'And now I'm going to ask you the same question.'

'My contract at Darjeeling has expired. Rather than renew it, I've decided to return home. In a few weeks time I shall join the Royal Army Medical Corps and be doing a more urgent job at the front in France. My wife and I are spending a week here, taking things easy before returning to Europe.'

'Good for you! I'm too old for the war.'

# Chapter 10

Gwendolyn now came into the conversation. 'The four of us are staying in Colombo for only a few hours. We came ashore this afternoon from the SS *Simla* to visit the city. We're leaving again tomorrow.'

'Four? What four?' asked Dr Ballantyne, looking at his friend and Gwendolyn. But before she could answer, the young couple, who had just finished dancing, returned to their friends.

'Here are the other two,' said Gwendolyn, introducing them. 'Miss Ollis and Professor Oates.'

'A fine foursome,' exclaimed Dr Ballantyne. 'You're all going to be my guests for dinner this evening. The restaurant is really good.'

'Thank you, James,' said Dr Andrews. 'A cheerful evening on land after a fortnight of infernally hot days at sea is just what we needed.' The others too welcomed this suggestion warmly.

In the interval before dinner was served, Dorothy and Farley, making their excuses to their hosts, went into the garden for a walk, leaving their friends to talk about the good old days of their life in India.

It was a lovely balmy night, and a gentle breeze wafted Strauss's romantic melodies through the air. Farley took the light shawl that Dorothy was carrying on her arm and laid it on her shoulders. Then they took the main path that led to the fountain they saw lit up in the distance. When they reached it, Farley said, 'Here's a nice bench for a short rest before going on.' And they sat down. Farley took Dorothy's hand and looking fondly into her eyes, murmured to her, 'What I am about to say will come as no surprise to you. My feelings for you become deeper every day, and I don't want things to end when we arrive at Calcutta. Even though I think I read in your eyes and perhaps in your heart that you have some feeling for me, I would very much like to hear you say so. This would be a great gift to me and also a mutual bond.'

Dorothy, much moved, said nothing for a while. Then she answered, 'It's the first time anyone has spoken to me like that, and just when I had decided to take on a new life. That is the only thing that gives me cause for hesitation. Yes, I too feel the same as you do, and I'm happy to be able to tell you so.'

Farley, with his heart full of joy, kissed her tenderly without saying anything. Dorothy continued, 'I've entered into an obligation with Gwendolyn and her family for a year, and I don't want to go back on my word. I didn't think that at times sea voyages could be so dangerous ...'

Farley answered, 'Have no fear, darling; when we get to Calcutta, we shall have time to see each other and get to know each other better, and you'll honour your undertaking. The important thing is that we'll be able to meet often.'

Suddenly the two of them, coming back to reality, got up, exclaiming, 'The dinner! They're waiting for us.' They hurried back to the restaurant. Arriving on the veranda, they saw their friends sitting at a table laid for dinner, while the waiters were beginning to serve. Seeing them arrive, Dr Ballantyne muttered to his friends, 'What a nice couple!' When they were nearer, he exclaimed, 'Oh, here are the lovebirds. We were waiting for you before beginning.'

The dinner was excellent and passed off in a happy festive atmosphere. Dr Ballantyne made everyone feel at ease with his cheerfulness. Dorothy and Farley told him of the reasons that had induced them to go to India and their plans for the immediate future.

About half past ten the travellers took leave of their hosts to return on board the *Simla*. Dr Andrews asked his colleague, 'Send me news of the situation in France.'

'Certainly I shall,' said Dr Ballantyne. 'I'll write to you.'

It was a short walk to the *Simla*, as the hotel was quite near the harbour. On board there was still a certain amount of activity; in the saloon there was dancing in an atmosphere of festivity. But our friends, tired after their day on shore, said good night and went to their cabins. Gwendolyn, who had been rather silent during dinner, guessed something had occurred between Dorothy and Farley, but preferred not to say anything even when she was in the cabin with her friend. Dorothy told her that Farley had invited her to spend the morning till the time of the ship's departure at three the following afternoon, at Mount Lavinia Hotel to have a swim in the ocean.

Here Gwendolyn interrupted and asked, 'Where is this place?'

'About six miles from Colombo. Farley has already been there on an

## Chapter 10

earlier voyage and says it's lovely. I'm sorry to leave you alone, Gwendolyn, but this will perhaps be our last chance to be alone before we get to India. After the swim we'll have lunch in the hotel and be back in time for the departure.'

'Don't worry about me, my dear. Dr Andrews and I had already thought of spending the morning shopping in Colombo. We'll meet again on board before the ship sails.'

## Chapter 11

The whole group met early the following morning for breakfast. Dorothy and Farley left hurriedly and went ashore in a boat waiting to pick up passengers. On arriving at the quayside they took a taxi to the Mount Lavinia Hotel.

This hotel commanded a splendid view. It was built on a headland, rich in vegetation and palm groves, overlooking a bay well sheltered from the strong ocean currents, which was therefore a good place for bathing. Even the sharks were kept at a safe distance by protective netting. It was a well-known spot, popular at all times of the year. Dorothy was in raptures from the very first moment. Farley kept the taxi so that it should be available for the return journey. Then the two young people ran down to the beach. The water was warm and a positive invitation to swim. They spent the morning in this way, swimming, basking in the sun and enjoying life.

Dorothy was wearing a long striped costume, in fashion at that time, rather similar to a coat, but for the first time she felt free and as happy as a child. Farley followed her as she came out of the water and ran towards the sand dunes, which were dotted with tufts of tall grass and a few palms. Hot from running she flung herself down in the shade of a palm tree and Farley joined her. Suddenly the two clung together in a passionate embrace. It was a moment of great joy and tenderness. Time seemed to stop still.

The ocean was gently ruffled by the breeze into little crests of foam. Light white clouds floated in the sky in ever changing shapes. Suddenly the couple came down to earth. Arm in arm they made their way slowly towards Mount Lavinia Hotel. It was lunchtime. They ate on a rather crowded veranda, which a lush awning of tropical plants shaded from the rays of the burning sun. After lunch they returned, somewhat reluctantly, to the taxi for the journey back to Colombo. They had not covered more than a mile or two, however, when a puncture forced them to stop. But the operation of putting on the spare wheel in place of the other took such a long time that the two began to get worried, afraid that they would arrive too late to catch the ship. In God's good time the job was finished, but before setting off again the taxi driver with a broad smile said to Farley, 'Wheel no good, sahib, too old. I go slow.'

In answer to this observation, Farley said, 'I told you we had to catch the ship that's leaving at three.' The poor fellow smiled disarmingly and said nothing.

The rest of the journey was spent in a growing tension for fear of further disasters. They arrived at the quayside at 3.10 in a state of extreme agitation. They looked towards the ship, expecting to see it on its way, but they were very surprised to see it still at its berth and showing no sign of imminent departure. They ran to a boat and Farley shouted, 'Quick, to the *Simla*.' Their agitation did not lessen till they were on the deck of the ship, where they saw Gwendolyn quietly stretched out on a deck chair reading a book. When she saw them arrive still in a state and breathless, she was worried and asked, 'What's the matter with you?'

'Wasn't the ship due to sail at three?'

Gwendolyn, coming down to earth, answered, 'The departure has been put off till seven this evening. Didn't you know?'

Dorothy and Farley looked at each other, bewildered and wide-eyed, and the burst into loud laughter, which at long last broke the accumulated tension. Gwendolyn, seeing them laugh, laughed too. Then Dorothy told her what had happened on the return journey from Mount Lavinia Hotel.

The atmosphere at dinner was euphoric. Everyone had lots to tell after their first contact with the Far East. Lilly and Jessica, especially, were taken aback at their first sight of rickshawmen and spoke endlessly about them. Lilly said, 'We spent the morning at the Galle Face Hotel, where we were invited by our friends. The hotel is a little out of Colombo in a lovely position overlooking the sea.'

At this point Dorothy interrupted, 'We also spent the morning in a lovely place, Mount Lavinia Hotel, where we were able to swim in the ocean. Luckily the trip did not turn into a real disaster, as the sailing time had been postponed.' She then told again the story of what had happened, to the huge amusement of the girls.

## Chapter 11

Jessica said, 'We didn't have any accidents of this sort, as Freddie and Toby took rickshaws.'

'We're not in London here,' added Dr Andrews, 'And Farley and Dorothy had to pay the penalty for using modern means of transport!'

Then Lilly went on, 'But you didn't see the sensitive plants that close up when they are touched. There were some lovely ones in the spices garden, where Freddie took us. He's a biology expert and was very keen to see them. It was a really interesting experience for us as well.'

Dr Andrews turned to Gwendolyn and said, 'Why don't we invite Jessica's and Lilly's young men to our table?'

Gwendolyn agreed with a smile, and the two girls exclaimed delightedly, 'Oh good, we would be very pleased.'

Dr Andrews gave orders to the steward to have their table set for eight as from the next day.

The last four days on board ship saw nothing new in particular, except for the Farewell Gala evening, which took place on the last day but one, and the Captain's Dinner on the final evening. The committee worked hard to make the Gala really unforgettable. Once again Dorothy was asked to take part, playing at the beginning and end of the show. While Dr Andrews and the other committee members were settling the details of the programme, they were approached by a distinguished middle-aged gentleman, who asked to speak to them. He said, 'I'm a professional actor and I'm going with my wife and another couple of actors to join a Shakespeare company that is at present performing in Calcutta. After that we shall all go on tour to several of the big cities. We shall be very pleased to take part in the Gala.'

The Purser, who was chairing the committee meeting, said, 'We shall be delighted to accept your kind offer and would be glad to know what you would like to perform.' The actor answered, 'At the moment we've got two scenes ready, one from *Hamlet* and the other from *Romeo and Juliet*, and, if there's time, a modern comic sketch.'

The offer was warmly accepted, as it would provide novelty to the evening. Farley also offered his contribution: he would read a new poem written at Colombo and inspired by his rickshaw ride there and consequently called *Rickshawman*. The programme was completed with the usual games, riddles, quizzes and a sweepstake. These items would allow fine prizes to be won.

It was a foregone conclusion that the Gala was an enormous success, in view of the previous similar evenings. At the end an army colonel went up on to the stage and in the name of all the passengers gave heartfelt thanks to all those that had performed during the Gala evening and who, by means of their art, had enabled everyone to get through some difficult moments. This led him on to some patriotic reflections on the present situation in England and France. He concluded, 'Never forget that we're English ...'

Suddenly the voice of Dr Andrews was heard, 'Not me! I'm Scottish.'

The audience laughed and applauded this interruption. The colonel corrected himself, 'We're all British – excuse me – and we must hold our heads high, especially in India, where it behoves us to set a good example.'

This speech, which was in tune with what was generally felt, aroused loud applause. Then everyone got up and without prompting broke into *God save the King* accompanied on the piano by Dorothy.

The audience, somewhat naturally, regarded the singing of the nation anthem as the end of the festivities and began to drift off. The colonel, however, who was taken aback by the interruption to his speech, raising his voice a little, went on, 'I will conclude by saying ...' and stopped, while the audience looked at him in embarrassed uncertainty and shuffled back to their seats and sat down. When the colonel felt he had the attention of the audience once again, he resumed his speech. 'I will conclude by giving you some advice.'

'Heavens! When will the old bore stop?' was the secret thought of many.

'It is this. Fear no man! Do right. Fear all women. Don't write.'

It was the turn of the audience to be taken aback by this sudden switch from turgid moralizing to a dreadful pun, and they laughed and clapped. This time they knew the colonel had finished, as he had already left the stage almost before they were aware of the fact.

The following evening was a mixture of joy and sadness; joy because once more everyone was together in a friendly atmosphere over an

## Chapter 11

excellent dinner, and sadness because everyone wondered what was in store for them after their arrival in India. There were promises to meet again and an exchange of addresses ...

The feature of the last day's sailing was a heavy and persistent rain – it was almost the end of the monsoon – with a high temperature and a long swell that gave rise to numerous cases of queasiness among the passengers. However it was not established for certain whether this was due, not so much to the weather conditions, as rather to the copious dinner of the previous evening, or perhaps to both. The radio brought the news that it was very hot in Calcutta and that the mosquitoes were troublesome. For all these reasons the euphoria of the previous evening was much reduced. About midday the *Simla* entered muddy water, indicating the proximity of the mouth of the Ganges. Getting over their queasiness, many passengers went on deck the better to witness the arrival of the *Simla*. About five o'clock the first shout of 'Land!' was heard and the news spread rapidly throughout the ship. An hour later the ship stopped to take the pilot on board; it was his job to sail the ship up the Hugli, one arm of the Ganges delta, to Calcutta. However to the great disappointment of the passengers, the ship did not proceed on its course but cast anchor where it then was. It was made known that it was too dangerous at night to sail up the Hugli, which is one of the most dangerous rivers in the world on account of the ever-shifting sandbanks. The ship would proceed at dawn the next day and was due to arrive at Calcutta at five in the afternoon.

Calcutta is about seventy miles from the sea on the banks of the river Hugli, one of the countless arms of the Ganges delta. The Hugli is in its own right a substantial river, nearly half a mile wide, which can provide anchorage to ships of all sizes.

Many passengers on the *Simla*, those that were going to India for the first time, were surprised to learn that it needed another eight or nine hours to reach Calcutta. But once they were in the river, they realized why, because they saw the ship twisting and turning as it went slowly upstream against the rapid current and the ever-moving shoals.

After lunch the *Simla* passed vast rice paddies that were visible on both sides and at last came in sight of the city. The passengers had for some time now been crowding the decks to enjoy the sight of the river full of boats and the city with its commercial buildings. It was like London again. It had in fact been the capital of British India till 1912. Finally the ship berthed at Quay number 4. Many of the passengers, looking at the wharf, called out 'Papa, Mummy', or various other names of people that they recognized.

Farley said, 'You're lucky if you've got someone waiting for you. The first time I arrived here, there was no one for me, and I wasn't very happy. This time, I hope, things are different. Right, Dorothy?'

Gwendolyn had for some time been looking at the crowd of people milling on the quayside. Suddenly, losing all her usual British phlegm, she shouted out, 'Liam, Liam, here I am!' And then taking off her topee she began waving it frantically. Dorothy copied her. From the land there suddenly came an answering flutter of handkerchiefs: from Major Waterhouse, his son David and his grandson Alan, who thus made their presence known. As soon as the gangway was hoisted in place, they went onboard to welcome Dorothy and Gwendolyn. Liam took his wife on his arms and squeezing her tight said, 'How glad I am, darling, to see you again. The months while you were away have seemed so long.' Gwendolyn gave him an equally warm answering embrace and said, 'I have been looking forward to this moment. This is Miss Ollis, whom I've spoken about in my letters.' Then, picking up her grandson and kissing him, she added, 'How you've grown and how heavy you are, Alan. Miss Ollis is going to be your governess.' Little Alan very politely took the hand Dorothy offered him.

'What about me, mama? Don't I get a kiss?' said David, smiling at Gwendolyn.

'Of course you do, darling.' And Gwendolyn clasped her son and kissed him.

Farley and Dr Andrews, who had remained a little in the background during the family meetings and greetings, now came forward and Gwendolyn made the introductions.

'Liam dear,' she said to her husband, 'These two gentlemen have been most useful to us during the voyage and have helped us through some difficult moments on shipboard. I hope that you will invite them to our house as early as possible.'

## Chapter 11

The group continued to chat, sitting in a shady spot on the deck, while they waited for the luggage to be taken on shore.

Dr Andrews went on, 'Many thanks for your invitation. I shall be delighted to visit you at some other time. But for now I must join my regiment immediately in Darjeeling. I leave tomorrow.'

'Why don't you come to dinner with us this evening,' exclaimed Liam. 'And you too of course, Mr Oates.'

'What a good idea,' said Gwendolyn. 'I hadn't thought of that. We shall expect you at eight.'

Meanwhile Lilly and Jessica went by, accompanied by their brother and the two young men. There were introductions all round, and Gwendolyn took the opportunity of wishing the two girls a very happy stay in Patna, hoping to see them again in Calcutta before they returned to England. The group broke up and all the passengers began to land, as the signal had been given for the luggage to be accompanied through the customs.

After these formalities the cases were loaded on to the carriage and the Waterhouse family and Dorothy set off for Government House. Farley and Dr Andrews took a taxi to the Great Eastern Hotel, one of the best in the city.

## Chapter 12

As the carriage approached Government House, Dorothy was wide-eyed at the size of the place. Liam, seeing the amazement of the girl, explained to her, 'Perhaps you don't know that till two years ago this was the residence of the Viceroy and the centre of the government of India. It has now become the residence of the Governor of Bengal, because the central government has moved to New Delhi. I, as the Governor's advisor, have the right to live in the building with my family. As you see it is very big.'

'A lovely place,' commented Dorothy.

Meanwhile they reached the large wrought iron gate of the park, where two sentries of the palace guard were stationed. Their uniforms were so magnificent and their turbans so original that once again Dorothy was entranced. As the carriage went through, the two soldiers jumped to attention and saluted. Liam and his son gave an answering salute.

David said, 'These are the soldiers I am in command of, as an officer of the Governor's Guard. But I think their splendid salute was directed to the charming lady here present rather than to my father and me.' He smiled. Dorothy smiled too and blushed at the compliment.

In front of the palace entrance stood more than a dozen servants lined up and dressed in their best. For the third time Dorothy expressed her amazement. 'But are all these servants really yours?'

Gwendolyn replied, 'Dorothy, we're in India now, and everywhere you will find a superabundance of servants.'

When they alighted from the carriage, Gwendolyn, speaking in Hindustani, greeted all the servants individually and introduced Dorothy as the 'memsahib' who from then on would be part of the family. Then turning to Dorothy, she said, 'You must learn their language as soon as you can.'

The arrival of the two ladies with their quantities of luggage caused a certain amount of confusion in the house. But Gwendolyn made precise and rapid arrangements with a firm hand, and soon everything was in order.

Meanwhile David's wife, Marian arrived, accompanied by the ayah of Mary, the baby who was now nearly three, to welcome her mother-in-law and Dorothy. With these two Marian was cordial but a little reserved. This was explained by the fact that she was a typical representative of the Anglo-Saxon upper middle class, who had received a first class education at Cheltenham Ladies' College, where her character had been moulded by a Spartan regime and sport. The Waterhouse family, on the other hand was Welsh, and therefore Celtic, temperamentally passionate and emotional. This fact may also explain the immediate attachment between Gwendolyn and Dorothy, who was also Welsh.

The lady of the house took Dorothy to her little flat and then left her free to unpack her luggage with the help of a maid. The bedroom, which was large and airy, gave on to the park with its rich tropical vegetation, and the girl went at once to the window to admire the view: the garden below her was well tended and ablaze with flowers of every description. Dorothy decided she would take a walk in it the next day, perhaps with little Alan, when she would be less tired. The maid came in shortly afterwards, and Dorothy soon realized that all the English she knew was 'Welcome, memsahib'. So their conversation was very interesting, consisting of meaningful gestures and periods of silence. Nevertheless they understood one another! However from that moment Dorothy made up her mind to learn Hindustani as quickly as possible. When the luggage was unpacked, Shiraz brought tea to her in her room, so that she could then lie down before getting ready for dinner. Left to her own thoughts, Dorothy was overcome by many emotions and by her secret worries, so much so that for the first time she cried. But the thought of seeing Farley again soon restored her courage, and in a calmer state of mind she dropped off to sleep.

She was woken by Shiraz at about seven, just in time to get dressed for dinner. She chose a blue dress which brought out the colour of her eyes and gathered her long blond hair into a loose chignon that showed off her profile to good effect. She completed her toilette with a pearl necklace, given to her by her mother.

## Chapter 12

When Dorothy arrived in the drawing room, sherry had been served and Farley and Dr Andrews were drinking theirs with the family. Seeing her come in, the gentlemen got up and Liam said, 'Welcome, Dorothy. Shiraz tells us that you have had a little sleep. I'm sure you now feel better.'

Farley smiled at her with affection and Dorothy smiled back. She too was given a sherry, and then everyone moved into the dining room. The oval table was laid for seven persons, the two children having already eaten with the ayah and gone to bed. Liam and David were at the table ends, Dorothy and Farley on one side and Gwendolyn and Marian on the other with Dr Andrews between them.

The conversation during dinner was very lively. Liam at once asked Dr Andrews if he was still with the Bengal Lancers. 'I have heard a lot about you and your research into tropical illnesses. Now that you are back, what are you going to do?'

'Yes, for many years I was with the Bengal Lancers, but on reaching retirement age, I went home with the intention of spending the rest of my days there. But my plans made no allowance for my nostalgia for India ... So I have come back. I have been offered a less arduous job at Lebong, where I hope to be able to continue my work on tropical diseases.'

Dorothy asked, 'Where is Lebong?'

'It's a large military base near Darjeeling,' answered the doctor.

'Lucky you, my dear doctor,' exclaimed Farley. 'You won't have to sweat it out in the heart of Calcutta, but can enjoy the cool air of the Queen of the Hills. Isn't that what they call Darjeeling?'

'You're right, Farley,' said Gwendolyn. Then turning to Dorothy, she explained, 'In the hot season the whole Government and their families move up to Darjeeling. And so we shall have the pleasure of meeting Dr Andrews again. I'm sure you'll like Darjeeling, Dorothy.'

David, who so far had not said anything, now turned to Farley, 'And you, professor, where are you staying?'

'For the moment I'm at the Great Eastern Hotel. But a University colleague that I rang a short while ago informed me that there is a flat available at Middleton Row no. 10. I'm going to see it tomorrow. In fact I would like to ask these good ladies if they can go with me and give me the benefit of their experience.'

'Certainly,' replied Gwendolyn. 'I may be otherwise engaged, but Dorothy can definitely go with you.'

Liam now spoke. 'I have heard glowing reports of you, Mr Oates,' he said. 'I hope you decide to stay for a long time in India.'

Farley thanked Liam for his kind words and said that that was precisely his intention.

Now Marian spoke up, 'But why don't any of you tell us about your voyage and what you saw?'

'Let Miss Ollis speak,' suggested Dr Andrews. 'She was on her first voyage. We other three are now seasoned travellers.'

'I can't possibly tell you everything that happened in one month of sailing. All I can think of now is the stop off at Colombo. Farley and I were really afraid that the *Simla* had left without us. I still tremble when I think of that moment of panic.' And she told the story so amusingly that all the diners split their sides with laughter, especially when she described the young taxi driver, unflappable and seraphic.

David exclaimed, 'But did no one tell you of the delay in the sailing time?'

Gwendolyn answered slyly, 'Our two youngsters were in much too much of a hurry to get off the ship to listen to the announcements that were being made loud and clear.'

Dr Andrews, noticing the embarrassment of Dorothy and Farley, carried on, describing his meeting with his colleague, Dr Ballantyne, with whom they had dined and spent the evening at Colombo.

Then the conversation became general. Gwendolyn said to Liam, 'I haven't yet had the time to tell you that we have at the table three artists: a great pianist, a poet and a clever conjuror.'

'Who's the poet?' asked Marian, looking alternately at the two guests.

Farley answered, 'I'm no poet. I only write verses to amuse myself.'

Dr Andrews with a disclaimer said, 'And I'm no conjuror. When I was a student many years ago I learnt a few tricks to while away the long Scottish evenings. In comparison with us Miss Ollis is a real professional.'

At this point Liam said, 'Miss Ollis, if you're not too tired, would you be willing to play something after dinner?'

## Chapter 12

Dorothy agreed readily.

Coffee and liqueurs were served in the drawing room, where a large Bluthner piano was on show. Dorothy admired the instrument, went up to it, sat down and began to play from memory a Chopin waltz. When the music was over, there was a moment's silence, then a burst of applause from those present, who included the servants, who were attracted by the sound of music and listened to the concert hidden behind the curtains of the drawing room door. Dorothy, her face red with excitement, returned to her place beside Farley, who got up gallantly and kissed her on the hand.

Liam, overcome with enthusiasm, exclaimed, 'From now on every one of our soirees will be a triumph.'

'If Dorothy agrees to take part,' added Gwendolyn diplomatically.

Dorothy then said, 'But who has played this splendid instrument till now?'

'No one,' they answered in chorus. 'We were waiting for you.'

So the evening came to an end. Dr Andrews made his farewell to the family, saying, 'Thank you once again for the lovely evening. I hope to see you all at Darjeeling during the holidays.'

Farley too gave his thanks for the pleasant evening and said he would come in the morning to pick up Dorothy and Gwendolyn and show them the flat he was thinking of taking.

# Chapter 13

The next day was Saturday. Gwendolyn and Marian spoke to Dorothy in detail about the children and what they considered best for their upbringing, especially for Alan, who would be going to school the following year and to whom Dorothy would have to teach the elements of reading, writing and music.

Gwendolyn went on, 'Alan is an intelligent child and eager to learn, perhaps even too serious for his age. We would like him to play more and meet other children. It will be your job to look after him, especially in the morning, because in the heat of the afternoon the children have a rest and stay in their rooms with the ayah. So during that time you will be free to help me in the running of the house, and we shall also have some nice outings. We will enrol you in the Tollygunj Club. Even if you don't play golf you can spend your time there, walking, swimming or simply chatting to the many club members. We often go there with the children.'

Marian added, 'That is what you will be expected to do during the week. At the weekend you will be free to do what you like. You can go out on your own or you may prefer to spend the day with us. In any case our family usually goes to church on Sunday. We would be pleased if you did so too to set a good example to the children.'

Dorothy answered, 'That's fine for me. If any change were necessary for the sake of the children, we could talk about it. As for going to church, that's no problem.'

While the ladies' conversation was coming to an end, Farley arrived and was asked to wait in the drawing room till they were ready.

Gwendolyn and Dorothy hurried off to the drawing room. Seeing Farley, Gwendolyn said, 'Dear Mr Oates, I regret very much that I can't come with you, but after such a long time away from here, there are a thousand and one things for me to do, believe me. But you go off with Dorothy. You can tell me later what you have seen. Be a good guide for her and show her at least the European quarter of the city.

# The Queen of The Hills

I think this programme will keep you busy for the whole day. We'll expect you for dinner this evening.'

'You are very kind, Mrs Waterhouse, to look after Dorothy so well. This will make it easier for her to adapt to surroundings so different from England.'

Dorothy said, 'Just a moment while I get my bag,' and ran off. She came back, but Farley, seeing her hatless, said immediately, 'Where's you topee?'

Gwendolyn added, 'Never forget your topee. The sun is very dangerous here.' Dorothy obeyed, and the young couple went out.

The first thing they did was to take a rickshaw to Middleton Row to see the flat that Farley wanted to rent. It was to their liking, even though it was only a bachelor flat with centralized services. However it had the great advantage of being quite near Government House and so they would be able to meet frequently. Farley immediately signed the contract for one year and told the owner that he would move in as soon as possible.

'We are now free for the rest of the day,' he said to Dorothy. 'So I can show you something interesting.' He gave the rickshawman an order in Hindustani.

Calcutta in 1914 was not the vast megalopolis that it is today, swollen with tens of thousands of refugees, homeless and without work or hope. However in the streets in the city centre there was almost as much confusion as there is today: a jam of cars, trams, rickshaws, overloaded lorries in a lamentable state of repair, carriages, cyclists and pedestrians; all controlled by a policeman at every crossroads with varying degrees of success, and made more picturesque and original by the presence every so often of a cow that walked calmly through the general confusion, as if it knew that no one would dare touch it, being a sacred animal.

Farley and Dorothy's rickshaw wormed its way more or less dangerously through all the other vehicles till it reached the relative calm of a large impressive square, surrounded by splendid buildings and gardens.

Farley explained, 'This is Dalhousie Square, which can be regarded as the centre of the city. That is the post office,' and he pointed at a large building with an enormous dome on top.

## Chapter 13

They crossed the square without stopping and then took another street leading off it, which came out into another square, where Dorothy was surprised to recognize Government House on the right; in the morning light it looked to Dorothy like a fairy palace, all green and white.

'Yes,' said Farley. 'We've gone round in a circle. We'll get out of the rickshaw now, but we won't stop here. We'll take a tram to go to Tollygunj.'

'Gwendolyn was talking to me about it this morning. What is it? A golf club? I can't play golf.'

'Nor I. But there are lost of other things, you'll see. And on the way we'll be able to see lots of other interesting things.'

The tram ride was quite long and the tram crowded. Soon they saw a huge grass covered open space, where teams of young people were playing cricket.

Dorothy could not help exclaiming, 'Cricket? Here?'

'O yes!' answered Farley. 'The Indians are very keen on cricket, which they learnt from us. This place is called the Maidan, and is one of the green lungs of Calcutta.'

The tram stopped and many young men got off to join the players.

The golf club was out in the country at the tram terminus. On going into the park of the club, they saw a lush tropical vegetation. Dorothy was amazed to see a very large tree with a hundred trunks, or so it seemed. Farley, who was expecting this reaction, smiled and said to her, 'That is a banyan tree. You certainly won't have seen anything like it before. Its branches grow outwards and downwards to the ground, where they take root and become new trunks. I've seen some that cover an area with a diameter of more than thirty yards.'

They walked on, admiring the flowers and trees, many of which were not known to Dorothy. While they were on their walk, Farley saw coming towards him with a smile a university colleague.

'What a nice surprise,' said the newcomer. 'I thought you were still in England. When did you arrive? And who is this lovely lady? Introduce me.'

Farley, taken aback by this fulsome welcome, replied a little coolly, 'I arrived only yesterday. This is Miss Ollis, a friend who will stay for at least a year in India.' He added no further information. He was perhaps jealous of the rather wide-eyed and penetrating look that his friend was giving Dorothy. The man answered, 'Come and have a drink with me to celebrate your arrival.' And so they made their way to the clubhouse. They sat in the cool shade of the bar to have their drink and chatted till their lunch was served.

In the afternoon Farley decided to take Dorothy to Presidency College, where he taught, to show her round. So they took a launch which conveyed them across the Hugli. The college was still closed for the holidays; term began again in November. There was only the caretaker, who greeted them with great affability and gave them the keys so that they could move around more freely. They visited the Great Hall, the library, the staff room and then Farley took Dorothy into the classroom where he normally gave his lessons.

'For the moment this is my home, the place where I spend most of my time. I hope to be able to offer you something better, where we can always be together,' said Farley, putting his arm round her and touching her lips delicately with his.

Dorothy in a surge of tenderness answered his embrace and kiss warmly. But then she felt slightly embarrassed and said, 'It's getting late. We'd better go; I wouldn't like to be back late for dinner.'

On the way, Dorothy asked Farley, 'Isn't Middleton Row your home?'

'No, it's only a place to live temporarily. It's different.'

While they were re-crossing the river, they saw the *Simla*. Having taken on more provisions and coal and few passengers, it was setting sail again back to England. The two looked at each other; both of them felt a lump in their throats. They were a little bit homesick.

Meanwhile back at Government House Marian, taking advantage of Dorothy's absence, found a chance to speak to her mother-in-law about the new governess. Rather surlily she said, 'I think you treat her with rather too much familiarity. After all she is only an employee.'

'Does it not occur to you that behind those words of yours there is just a little bit of envy? Dorothy is quite an exceptional person, to be treated with the greatest respect. I had the fortune to get to know her very well during my months in England. For Clare too she was much

## Chapter 13

more than a secretary, more a trusted friend. She is a nice girl, intelligent, well educated and, not least, she comes from a good family. To be quite frank with you, I must tell you that I am very fond of her. So, my dear, I beg you to regard her as a member of the family, not as an employee. You won't regret it, believe me.'

And the conversation ended there.

Chapter 14

In 1912 Government House had become the official residence of the Governor of Bengal. With his family he occupied one entire wing of the large building. At the other end there were the government offices, the Headquarters of the Guard, under the command of Captain David Waterhouse, and the offices of Major Liam Waterhouse, Advisor to the Governor. There were also the respective private flats of the two high officials with their families, and other suites available for any guests. Dorothy occupied one of these. In the centre of the building there were the State Rooms, of which the Throne Room, as it was called when the Viceroy was in residence, was the most impressive. The Throne Room was used for the big official occasions and for receptions. The dining room was also very luxurious; this was used for official banquets. Not less luxurious were the numerous rooms intended for official visitors and conferences. The servants were housed in what were called godowns situated in the park. There they lived with their families.

Dorothy spent the morning in David and Marian's flat, where she had the use of a special room for Alan and herself next door to the nursery. Alan at once took a liking to her and was never tired of learning anything she taught him. His curiosity was especially directed to the animal world, above all to elephants. He had sometimes seen them in the parades of the Government House Guard. Dorothy promised to take him to the zoo where he would see wild animals as well. She taught him nursery rhymes that had animals in them, accompanying them with easy jingles that she played on the piano. Alan was much impressed with her playing and would come up to the piano, putting his hands on the keys in the hope of producing some chords.

Dorothy said to him with a smile, 'You will have to do a lot of study, my dear, before you can play.'

After lunch in David and Marian's flat and a short rest, Dorothy would go to Gwendolyn's for a few hours to help her in her social and charitable duties and meetings. Of real value to her now was the experience gained at Victoria College and everything that Clare had taught her. So Dorothy took advantage of a quiet evening to write a long letter to her dear friend, the Principal, telling her all about her new experiences.

In the evening, after checking that the ayah had seen to the children's supper and put them to bed, Dorothy would normally have dinner with Gwendolyn and her husband. She had chosen this solution offered her by Gwendolyn because she felt that the younger couple would prefer to be alone for dinner. Quite often too Farley was invited. Dorothy looked forward to these evenings with great pleasure, because a real family atmosphere had been established. Anecdotes and stories about the smart society of Calcutta were told; or they would play cards and very often Dorothy would play the piano for her friends. The young couple enjoyed being together and their affection for each other grew steadily. However more or less official dinners or parties were quite frequent, and these were served in the garden when the weather permitted, or if not, in the large dining room.

Dorothy's arrival had brought a wind of change into the uneventful and at times slightly monotonous life at Government House. Even David, the masterful Captain of the Guard, had been struck by the lively and exciting appearance of the young lady, whom a month spent on the *Simla* had tanned to a rich colour, very different from that of the ladies of Calcutta society. Shortly after her arrival Dorothy was invited as guest of honour to a little party given by the officers of the Government House Guard, under the command of David, together with their wives.

Everyone was eager to meet the newcomer, who had been spoken of in such glowing terms by David. When Dorothy arrived, wearing a simple dress of white silk with a yellow rose pinned to her décolletage and with her long blond hair flowing over her shoulders, they realized that there had been no exaggeration in the opinion given of her.

Marian (with some reluctance) and David went forward to greet her. 'My dear Dorothy,' said David, 'welcome to the Club of the officers of the Guard.' There was a universal cry of 'Hear, hear!' Dorothy thanked them with a smile. Then the party began and the officers and

## Chapter 14

their ladies came up one by one to be introduced. Lieutenant Frank Berry was among the last, because he was one of the youngest. He was very handsome, of above average height, and had dark hair and dark eyes, a piercing gaze and a rather enigmatic expression. He asked Dorothy, 'Are you staying here long, Miss Ollis? I've been told that you're a very good pianist. I'm a violinist. Could we play together sometimes?'

Dorothy was taken aback by this request, but attracted too by the charming address of the young man, as well as by his appearance. At first she was at a loss how to reply. In the end she said, 'I've only just arrived, lieutenant, and I think I shall be pretty busy, at least for the moment. Shall we see a bit later, when I am more organized?'

'I will wait patiently,' answered Frank.

In the following days Dorothy had occasion to meet Frank fairly often; in the garden, when she went out with the children, on the stairs and sometimes at the Waterhouses'. She did not know if these meetings were mere coincidence or if they young man was following her, but she was disturbed by his intense stare, which she did not know how to avoid. However Gwendolyn too had noticed the attentions that the lieutenant showed Dorothy, and one evening when Dorothy had lingered at dinner, Gwendolyn took her aside and said, 'Have you noticed that Lieutenant Berry has taken a fancy to you? The way he looks at you is pretty clear and he seeks ways and means of meeting you often.'

'Ways and means?' said Liam who came in at that moment. 'What's that supposed to mean?'

'Women's talk,' replied Gwendolyn with a smile.

'No, no, I want to know,' said Liam.

'Well, I think our Dorothy has broken another heart,' said Gwendolyn.

'Broken another heart?' said Liam, full of curiosity. 'Whose?'

Dorothy now spoke up, 'Lieutenant Berry.'

Liam added, 'A fine young man, intelligent as well as good looking.'

'Yes indeed, but he doesn't interest me, though I appreciate his good qualities.'

The next day a large bouquet of flowers was delivered to Dorothy, together with a letter. These Shiraz took up directly to Dorothy's room. When she came in after her lesson with Alan, she found them. She was amazed and moved when she read the words of fire that Frank had written to her, and during the rest of the day she pondered on what she should do, without solving the problem. She decided once more to seek the advice and help of Gwendolyn. After dinner that evening she gave her friend the letter to read that she had brought with her.

'Oh! Poor Frank!' exclaimed Gwendolyn. 'He's well and truly in love.' Then raising her eyes to look at Dorothy, she saw that she was crying.

'Why are you crying? Do you love him?'

'No, no. But I'm sorry for him, and I don't really know how to behave if I meet him. Give me some advice.'

Gwendolyn, who lacked neither determination or energy, said, 'Leave it to me. I will have a word with David.'

A few days later David called Lieutenant Berry into his office.

'What I'm going to say to you is as man to man, not as your commanding officer. You have arrived too late. The person to whom you have given your affection is not available and neither can nor wants to return it. You would be wise not to make difficulties for her.'

Frank was very upset at these words. He did not know what to say in reply and simply asked for permission to leave. He thought for a long time about what he should do. Finally he came to a decision: he would ask to be transferred to the Punjab Lancers, as he knew that this regiment was shortly due to leave for the front in France.

At dinner some days later, David said jokingly to Dorothy, 'You must be more careful. I don't want to lose any more good officers.'

Dorothy was at first abashed and lowered her eyes. But recovering her usual spirit, she replied, 'I will try my hardest from now on not to disturb the even tenor and peace of mind of your officers ...'

Some months later the news reached Calcutta that Frank had been wounded and sent back to England. The whole family Waterhouse and especially Dorothy were greatly distressed and wrote an affectionate letter of good wishes for a rapid recovery.

## Chapter 15

During the month that Farley spent before the beginning of the university term about the middle of November, he was busy partly in furnishing his new flat and partly in calling on people that were in Calcutta society, according to the custom of the period. In fact there was an absurd tradition that required that a young man who wanted to get into good Calcutta society should put on evening dress and a top hat, hire a carriage and go round personally delivering his visiting card to those persons by whom he wished to be received. Before performing this duty, he was not recognized socially. Fortunately this custom slowly died out when the 1914 war began. However, the Waterhouses were of great help to Farley during the period when he was settling in. They had lived in Calcutta for many years and, in view of the position that Major Waterhouse held, they knew all the people who were anybody in the city and the university.

In the following months both Farley and Dorothy were busy in their respective occupations. But they tried to meet as often as possible, in spite of this. Their attachment became ever deeper, more stable and lasting.

Every so often there were special occasions that allowed the young couple to be together for a longer time. They enjoyed going to Tollygunj Club to play tennis. Farley considered himself to be a passable player, but to his great surprise Dorothy beat him fairly often. Her style of game was defensive, determined and precise. She did not rely so much on lightning strokes, but more on a steady tenacity in her returns, so that her opponent became impatient at this style of game and made mistakes.

While they were having tea after the game, Farley said, 'I'm amazed to see how well you play. Where did you learn?'

Dorothy laughed; 'I was expecting that question. I learnt at school in Croydon. Tennis was part of the sporting tradition of the school, and I found I had an aptitude for it right from the start. I ended up in the school team. However there was one girl that I could never beat. She was a real champion. She was one of my best friends, and an Indian in fact.'

'That doesn't surprise me. The Indians have good ball sense. I also had a friend I could never beat, not however at tennis but in school. So I was always second in the class order. Tennis is not my sport. I'm a cricketer.'

In this way Farley was able to salve his *amour propre*.

About the end of November there was the annual 'Presentation' to the Governor of Bengal: a ceremony profoundly boring to all those taking part. It was however inconceivable that anyone receiving an invitation should decline to attend. This would have been a first class social gaffe. Among the hundreds of people invited there were the University teachers, and among these Farley. 'Academic dress' said the invitation, that is to say gowns and mortarboards.

The guests were crammed like sardines into the various anterooms to await their turn to be presented. At the door of each anteroom stood a gigantic Pathan in a splendid uniform: red turban, red tunic and white trousers. These Pathans came from the martial races that lived near the frontier with Afghanistan and formed the Government House Guard under the command of Captain Waterhouse. That day their duty was to control the flow of guests into the presence of the Governor. It was extremely hot in the overcrowded anterooms, and the queue advanced very slowly. People got impatient and began to push and jostle in order to be at the head of the queue. As a result there was more than one guest that was presented to the Governor, dishevelled with his gown askew if not actually torn. The Pathans stood there with inscrutable faces, and so nobody could know what was passing through their minds as they witnessed this undignified behaviour of the sahibs. The ladies were able to watch the ceremony from a gallery running high up round the Throne Room. Dorothy saw Farley arrive in front of the Governor. An official called out, 'Professor Oates'. He bowed, red faced from the heat, shook hands with the Governor and passed on. A matter of a few seconds ... Thus began Farley's social life.

About the middle of November Liam and Gwendolyn were given by the Governor the job of arranging the annual Christmas Gala. They

## Chapter 15

took great care over the list of names to submit to the Governor, as invitations to this Gala were much sought after and the number of them somewhat restricted to about eighty. The Governor gave his seal of approval with one or two minor alterations.

'Your Excellency', said Liam, addressing his superior, 'May I be allowed to keep secret the programme my wife and I are arranging? It will contain certain changes from that of previous years. However we are sure that you will not be disappointed.'

Sir Lionel Mitford answered, 'I know your wife too well to have any doubts about her judgement! I'm sure the programme will be a success. I thank you in advance for your efforts.'

Gwendolyn wasted no time in setting out her ideas to Dorothy. She asked her, 'Would you feel up to opening our Gala with a Beethoven sonata? This could be an excellent entrée for you into Calcutta society. Farley will also be among the guests as a friend of the family. Do you think we can count on his co-operation?'

'Why not?' replied Dorothy. 'He was a great success on the ship with his poems. I was also thinking of suggesting that Shakespearean Company that we heard on the ship and which should now be in Patna. They are a fine young group. As for myself,' she added, 'Beethoven will do very well. The Moonlight sonata doesn't need much introduction.'

'Two very good ideas. I'll ask Liam to find out the present whereabouts of those actors. A success here will be a good publicity boost for them in future.'

When Farley came to dinner that evening, the two ladies put before him their plans, and asked him what he thought about them. He found them excellent and undertook to read one of his most recent poems, adding, 'If you agree, let me recapitulate what you have told me. A buffet to begin the evening, then the show with music and acting. At the end dancing.'

'That's it,' said Gwendolyn, 'but please, don't talk to anyone about it, because it's a secret between us and must remain one.'

The days preceding the Gala were very busy for Gwendolyn and Dorothy. The former had to see to the buffet and the general arrangements for the evening. The latter was busy in the morning with Alan and in the afternoon she helped Gwendolyn, so that she had no time to devote to her favourite sport nor to seeing Farley. Fortunately he came fairly often in the evening and tried to help the ladies, at least with his advice, if nothing else.

'I've been told,' said Farley, 'that the actors have accepted our invitation. That's a relief.'

'I agree,' said Gwendolyn.

One evening Farley, who noticed Dorothy looking rather worried and tired when he said good night before leaving, said to her, 'Don't worry about the concert. Everything will go fine. I'm here near you and can help you.' And he embraced her tenderly. She thanked him with a kiss.

On the evening of the reception at about seven, most of the guests arrived more or less at the same time for fear of being late. So in front of Government House, all ablaze with lights, there was an indescribable jam of carriages, setting down ladies and gentlemen, the former in all their finery and bejewelled. In the latter there was a contrast: the civilians were in formal evening dress, the military in their splendid uniforms. But beggaring all description were the Indian guests. In particular the Maharajah and his wife provoked universal admiration; she was small and dainty in a white sari, embroidered with gold. She wore a costly necklace and turquoise earrings. The Maharajah, however, was tall and impressive. He was wearing a long coat of black velvet, embellished with jewels of many colours, and his black silk trousers were adorned with a golden stripe. On his head he had a purple turban with an enormous ruby in the centre and an ostrich feather at the side. He kept his turban on the whole evening in spite of the great heat. The other Indian couples had also put on their most splendid traditional wear.

The Governor, Sir Lionel Mitford, in full dress uniform, white silk with golden buttons and braid, stood with his wife at the top of the porch steps to welcome the guests. Immediately afterwards they were escorted into the dining room, where a sumptuous and variegated buffet awaited them on tables decorated with local flowers and fruit. Here Gwendolyn and Liam were doing the honours of the house and for each guest they had a greeting and a friendly word.

## Chapter 15

There was a great surprise when at nine o'clock the major-domo announced, 'My lords, ladies and gentlemen, be pleased to take your seats in the Throne Room for the entertainment.' Gwendolyn, aware of a certain whispering and muttering due to curiosity, asked the guests for a moment's silence to give them some explanation, 'My dear friends, we have made some changes from the usual programme. I am sure you will have an enjoyable evening and not be disappointed.'

The guests clapped, although a little puzzled, and went off to the Throne Room.

Before the beginning of the concert, Dorothy was so nervous that she could not touch the food, however delicious it was. Not even the proximity of Farley who was ever beside her could calm her. At last she heard Liam's announcement, 'I have great pleasure in introducing to you Miss Dorothy Ollis, who will play for you Beethoven's Moonlight Sonata.' From the very first notes the listeners were aware that they were in the presence of a real artist and the silence was total.

At the end the audience's reaction fulfilled Gwendolyn and Liam's highest hopes for the success of the evening. Dorothy too was quite overcome with emotion when she saw a valet bring her an enormous bouquet of flowers. Liam mounted the platform and said, 'On behalf of the Governor and his illustrious guests we thank you for the moments of real emotion that you have given us. We hope that there will be other occasions to listen to you in future.' There was further applause in the hall. While the servants were removing the piano, Liam went on, 'May I now introduce to you Professor Oates, who will read you his poem, *The Rickshawman.*' After the success this poem had had on the *Simla,* Farley thought that it would not be amiss to repeat it on this occasion too before a more sophisticated audience. He went up on to the platform and explained, 'These verses are the fruit of a day spent in a rickshaw in Colombo.'

With his ringing and well-modulated voice, Farley managed to make the reading lively and amusing. The applause at the end, combined with the laughter, was proof that he had succeeded.

Liam came forward once more and announced, 'For the last item in our show, ladies and gentlemen, the new travelling Shakespeare Company will perform two short scenes: the first from *Romeo and Juliet,* the second from *The Taming of the Shrew.*'

There was an immediate buzz of approval. The Governor, who had Gwendolyn sitting next to him, whispered to her, 'What a wonderful idea, Mrs Waterhouse.' And Gwendolyn blushed at the compliment.

The spectators' appreciation of the young actors was due, not only to their undoubted talent, but also to the fact that many of those present had not for a long time had the chance to see such a performance. They were reminded of the time in their youth when they too had performed in the school play.

At the end of the show Liam announced, 'Ladies and gentlemen, as soon as the hall has been rearranged, the dancing will begin. In the meantime, for those that wish, the buffet is still open, or you may walk in the garden or elsewhere.'

As the Governor got up he said to Gwendolyn, 'I haven't been introduced to the young pianist, Miss Ollis I think she is called. I don't know Professor Oates either. Will you introduce them to me?'

Gwendolyn made haste to have them summoned. They were eating at the buffet, calm at last after the agitation of the evening.

Introducing them, Gwendolyn said, 'Here are the mainstays of our show. Miss Ollis, a dear friend, arrived from England a few months ago to take care of our grandson, Alan. We hope she will stay here for a long time,' and she looked at Farley with a smile. She then went on, 'And Professor Oates had been teaching history now for a few years at Presidency College. He was on the same boat with us out from England, where he spent a few months holiday.'

The Governor congratulated both of them on their excellent performance. 'I hope we may count on you on some future occasion.'

Farley replied, 'We shall be delighted, your Excellency.'

While the couple were moving away, Liam approached with the actors. These also conversed with the Governor for a few minutes.

Some friends of Gwendolyn and Liam wanted to congratulate them on the great success of the show and the original idea of holding it. Gwendolyn answered, 'It's not my idea. It grew out of a group of friends that I spent a long month travelling with on the *Simla*.'

While they were talking, the servants finished arranging the hall. The orchestra struck up with *Antonio*, a tune that was all the rage at that time. Farley took Dorothy by the hand and asked her to dance.

Chapter 16

On Christmas Eve, Farley asked Liam and Gwendolyn if he could speak to them privately. They met while Dorothy was busy with Alan.

'My dear friends, I would like to ask you for the hand of Dorothy, as you are her surrogate parents. I have promised her that I will wait a year before marrying her, but in the meantime I would like to offer her a pledge of my love; tomorrow I will give her an engagement ring. For the moment I think it would be better not to let this news go any further for the sake of Dorothy, who wants, before anything else, to inform her parents in England. We shall make the engagement official, if you agree, before you leave for Darjeeling in May.'

'We're absolutely delighted at this news,' said Liam. Gwendolyn added, 'You're a splendid couple and we wish you every happiness. We shall offer you a lovely party in the garden for your official engagement. We're also glad that Dorothy will remain with us for some months more, but we certainly don't want to stand in her way if she wants to make her own life and be happy.'

The next day, Christmas Day, the whole family, Dorothy and Farley were gathered in Gwendolyn's drawing room. In a corner by the window a small palm tree had been festooned as a Christmas tree. Under it were a number of beautiful coloured parcels for everyone. Dorothy too found her parcels. She opened the smallest, which contained a little box, and in it there sparkled a ring mounted with an emerald and a circle of diamonds. It was only when she read the note that went with it that she realized the significance of the gift. She blushed to the roots of her hair and, rushing impulsively to Farley, she kissed him. David and Marian, who were not *au courant* with the new situation, were greatly surprised. Alan, in his childish naivety, exclaimed, 'Are you getting married, Miss Ollis? I thought you would always stay with me,' Dorothy answered, 'I shall be staying for some time more, Alan, but not for ever.' Liam informed David and Marian of the news, adding that for the moment it must remain a secret at Farley's request.

During the Christmas dinner David made a warm toast to the pair and added, 'It's a pity, though, that we shall be losing a very good governess.' Marian simply nodded.

The family spent the Christmas break quietly. In the afternoon the ladies would go with Dorothy and the children to Tollygunj Club to meet their friends and let the children play freely. One day Alan asked Marian: 'You once promised me that we would go on a nice trip into the country. When will we be going, mummy?'

'We can ask daddy to help us get ready for it, because we need horses and also an elephant to take us.'

Dorothy spoke up, 'But I can't ride.'

'It will be useful for you to learn,' Marian said to her, 'because in India it is essential. But don't worry. It's not difficult. Also Farley can teach you. He's a good rider.'

David, prompted by his wife, gave orders for the servants to make arrangements for an excursion lasting five days. Preparations of this sort, even for a small family group, were no small matter. Some servants went ahead of the sahibs with food, equipment and tents, which were then set up at the chosen place. When the party arrived on horseback or on the elephant, everything was ready and all that the sahibs had to do was to sit down and eat.

The day fixed for the start Liam and his wife, David and Farley were on horseback, while Marian, Dorothy and the children travelled on the elephant. Dorothy had opted for this solution, not only because Alan wanted to have her near, but also because she feared that she would not be able to ride for long the first time.

The group advanced at a steady pace. There is no hurrying an elephant and the horses walked at the same speed. They arrived at the place previously chosen for lunch, a clearing near a village on the edge of the jungle. The servants had already prepared everything. Nothing was left for Gwendolyn to do but order the lunch to be served at once. The children were tired. Mary was carried off straight to bed, but Alan was too excited by the novelty and wanted to stay with the grown ups in spite of his tiredness. David urged Dorothy not to let Alan go off alone because dangerous animals could be lurking in the high grass.

## Chapter 16

The lunch was as always rich and copious, and everyone ate with gusto. After a short siesta David mooted the idea of going to visit the neighbouring village, where there lived the family of one of the Government House guards that he knew very well.

Meanwhile the news of their arrival had spread, and some of the village elders had arrived during lunch to greet the sahibs and the memsahibs, bringing them fruit and flowers.

The village consisted of a few dozen bamboo huts, neat and clean. When the party arrived at Namud's home, his wife, accompanied by the entire quite numerous family, including all the in-laws, came out to meet the group and welcome them. They said 'Salaam', bowing and joining their palms together in front of their chests. David and the others answered in the same way. The women invited them in, and they accepted. Marian, speaking in Bengali, said, 'I should very much like to see the beautiful cloth that you and your daughters are weaving on the loom.' Then they went in and saw one of the girls, who was sitting on the ground and working at the loom. There were neither chairs nor tables. Only a carpet covered the floor.

Dorothy was amazed and charmed seeing the skill of the girl. This was her first contact with the real India. She said at once to Marian that she would like to buy some towels for her trousseau. Gwendolyn interrupted, 'Let them be a gift from me to you.' Marian ordered two tablecloths, one for herself and one for Dorothy, who was overcome by the generosity of the two ladies and thanked them.

When they were on the point of leaving the hut, two peasants ran in and began an agitated conversation with the sahibs. Seeing everyone looking worried, Dorothy asked Farley, 'What's the matter?'

'They have brought news that last night in the next village a calf was killed by a tiger. They are asking for our help to kill it. They have great confidence in our prowess as hunters, and we must not disappoint them.'

So there was a change in the programme. Marian and Dorothy and the children were escorted back to the camp, notwithstanding the protests of Alan, who wanted to go with his father 'to kill the tiger'.

Liam, David, Farley and Gwendolyn (women too hunted alongside the men) took their rifles, got on their horses and rode off to the village, accompanied by the peasants and some servants.

The group left their horses in the village and made their way on foot into the jungle, following the tracks of the tiger. They were not hard to find: the creature had dragged the dead calf away before eating it, but it had then abandoned it half eaten in an open space among the trees. The hunters were therefore sure that the tiger would come back to finish its meal. They were ever on the watch both for the tiger and for poisonous snakes that infested the jungle. They decided to lie in wait for the tiger, each one sitting in a safe place in the branches of a tree. They could see each other but could only communicate by signs. If the animal returned by nightfall, so much the better. If not, they would leave their hiding places to return at dawn the next day. The dusk came on and they were on the point of coming down from the trees, when David and Farley heard the cracking of undergrowth among the low bushes, and they made signs to the others to stay put, pointing in the direction of the noise. In spite of the darkness Liam and Gwendolyn saw the signal and listened. Then the creature, a huge male Bengal tiger came out and advanced on its prey. Two rifle shots rang out almost simultaneously and the animal fell, killed outright. The four clambered quickly down from the tree, stiff after their long wait. They walked prudently towards the animal and examined it. There were two wounds, one in the head and the other, a superficial one, on the shoulder. The latter alone had hardly grazed the skin. The other shot, however, was fatal. Suddenly a single thought passed through the minds of Farley and David – which of the two had fired the fatal shot? In haste Farley said craftily to David, 'We killed the tiger, didn't we?'

'We did,' replied David, poker faced.

Thus the mystery remained, as both were perfect gentlemen.

Then it was essential to get out of the jungle as soon as possible and return to camp. So they had to leave the animal where it was for the night. They would give orders the next day to have it flayed and made into a rug. It was pitch dark when they reached the camp, where the ladies were quite worried by the long time they were away.

Alan, who had waited all afternoon for the return of the hunters, had been overcome by sleep. The two ladies, however, wanted to know all the details of the hunting adventure. Dorothy was quite upset. 'Do you often see tigers in India?'

*Chapter 16*

Farley answered, 'Not often. They stay in the jungle unless they are hungry. But to kill them you need to have a good rifle and be very careful.'

The next morning Alan at once asked, 'Where's the tiger?'

His father answered, 'We killed it, but now it has to be skinned. You will see it when it has been made into a nice carpet.'

The child accepted the explanation but was not altogether satisfied.

The rest of the trip had to be modified on account of what had happened, but there were no further incidents. Farley took advantage of these few days to teach Dorothy to ride. Alan too had his first experience on a little pony with his father holding the bridle. Both Dorothy and Alan were delighted with this new sport, which they could practise at Calcutta as well. The party returned to the city as the holidays were nearing their end everyone had to start work again.

## Chapter 17

Dorothy resumed her lessons with Alan, who was learning quickly and in a short time he could read. He also like music and would often sing little tunes or nursery rhymes with Dorothy and with his mother. The latter was very pleased with the progress Alan had made since Dorothy's arrival. Her initial reserve in her relations with the governess had disappeared, to Gwendolyn's great delight.

At the beginning of February the Governor gave Liam the job of organizing a party on the Hugli for Alan's fifth birthday. He added, 'This will be my birthday present to him. I should like you to hire a nice houseboat to invite all the small children of the Government House staff.'

'That's very kind of you, Your Excellency. I'm sure Alan will be pleased.'

No sooner said than done. On 24 February, Alan's birthday, a score of little boys and girls, accompanied by their mothers, sat down round a large table laid for them on the houseboat, laden with food and sweets, which proved very popular with them all. To make the party more enjoyable a group of Indian jugglers, conjurers and acrobats had been invited for the afternoon. These were geniuses at involving the children; one of them found a dove on his head, another a rabbit in his arms or a cat in a basket. But the excitement knew no bounds when there appeared a tiger cub, which naturally all the children wanted to cuddle. But the cub disappointed as quickly as it had appeared. To compensate for the children's disappointment, each one was given a biscuit shaped like a tiger. There was a wild general applause from both children and adults. Dorothy, for whom it was the first time at such an entertainment, enjoyed herself enormously.

When they reached home, Alan, still excited and enthusiastic about the day out, wanted to tell his parents and grandparents about everything that had happened. But suddenly he went pale and began to tremble. Dorothy took him up in her arms and rushed him off to bed.

They took his temperature: 102 degrees. Marian and the rest of the family were aghast. The doctor was called and he came very quickly. 'Chickenpox', he decreed. 'This is my third case today.' Then he wrote out the appropriate prescriptions. David thought it advisable to inform the parents of the children that were at the party, but some of these were already ill. Even Marian and Dorothy had to remain in quarantine for a week. So Farley wrote a letter to Dorothy every day. She replied to him immediately to keep him informed. After a week Farley received a message, 'Danger over. We are expecting you this evening.' And life started again as usual.

Nothing important happened in March and April. The temperature climbed inexorably. Social life came to an end, as usual, in March, when the young ladies that had arrived in the autumn for the 'season' – the so-called Fishing Fleet – went home to England, at least those who had not hooked a husband. Everyone had to prepare themselves psychologically for the onset of the Hot Weather, except for the upper grades of Government servants with their families and any others who could find ways and means of getting out of Calcutta. These lucky ones, every year about the middle of May, would move *en bloc* up to Darjeeling and stay there till the end of September.

Darjeeling, at seven thousand feet above sea level, was a tiny village of fifty inhabitants till 1860, when the British discovered it and turned it into the 'Queen of the Hills', a name which it retains to this day. In a few decades the fifty inhabitants became fifty thousand. This increase occurred for three good reasons. The first was the planting of tea, started by the British, and this needed a large labour force. The second was the discovery that Darjeeling had a climate that was ideal for holidays: cold but sunny in winter, warm but rainy in summer. And finally, a railway was built, sixty miles long, from the railhead at Siliguri in the plain up to Darjeeling, a marvel of engineering, with small trains running on a track with a two foot gauge round and round the mountain with very sharp curves.

The town is all up and down. From any point in Darjeeling the view is magnificent. The chain of the Himalayas with its snow-capped peaks rises to the north in a vast semicircle, culminating in the sharp peak of Kanchenjunga. There are only two level spaces, the railway station

# Chapter 17

and the Chowrasta, meaning 'Six Roads', where six roads converge. One of these led off at that time to Government House, where the Governor of Bengal, his family and all his staff with their families, moved to in May.

During these days Gwendolyn, helped by Marian, Dorothy and some of the maids, organized everything that was necessary for the move to Darjeeling. As always, several of the servants were sent on in advance, so that everything should be in running order when the sahibs arrived.

Farley, who was still busy at the university for the next fortnight, would arrive in Darjeeling at the end of term early in June and he would stay in the hills till early in July, when the next term, the monsoon term, would begin. Liam had kindly offered to let him live for that time in Government House, where there were many free rooms. David, however, had to remain in Calcutta with the Guard and would only see the family again for a short break about the end of June.

On arrival in Darjeeling, Dorothy and the children did not feel well for a few days. Dorothy was afraid she was seriously ill and confided her fears to Gwendolyn.

'Nothing to cause alarm,' said the older lady. 'It's the effect of the altitude. It will pass off in a couple of days. The children also have the same problem. As you see, we are not worried.' And Dorothy was reassured. In fact in a few days both she and the children had completely recovered.

The first week was taken up with the resumption of social contacts: visits, parties and dinners. The climate, so cool and fresh, invited one into the garden or onto the terrace. Many people opted for long walks in the crisp and sunny mountain air. They were making the most of the few short weeks before the onset of the monsoon and were as much as possible in the open air.

One day Dorothy had gone out with Alan to explore the bazaar, which fascinated both of them because of all the wonderful things they could find there. They had heard a lot about it. As they were walking, Dorothy suddenly heard a loud cry, 'Dorothy!' She turned round. 'Agnes!' she exclaimed. 'What are you doing here?'

'I might ask you the same question.'

Before answering each other, the two ladies embraced one another warmly. That created a considerable stir, mixed with a feeling almost of bewilderment, among those near by, both Europeans and Indians. It should be said at once that Agnes was not European but Indian, and in 1915 such a close and obvious personal friendship between persons of the two different races was looked on askance by both groups.

Dorothy spoke first: 'Alan, this is Miss Mukerji. She and I were at school together in England. She was my best friend and still is, though I could never beat her at tennis.' Then turning to Agnes, she went on, 'I am Alan's governess. He's the grandson of Major Waterhouse, advisor to the Governor.'

Alan was mystified that the ladies could ever have been at school together. He opened his eyes wide, but as children of five have no racial prejudice (they learn it later from adults), he said very politely and without prompting, 'Good morning, Miss Mukerji.'

Agnes answered, 'I'm very pleased to meet you, Alan.' Then to Dorothy she added, 'I'm not Miss Mukerji any more, you know. Five years ago I became Mrs Majumdar; I've got a daughter of four and a son of two.'

'Congratulations', said Dorothy warmly. 'Give me your address at once. We must see each other again and renew contacts.'

Agnes did so and the two friends went their separate ways.

As Dorothy and Alan continued their walk, the boy asked, 'Why did the lady go to school in England?'

'Her father is quite rich, so he and Agnes's mother wanted her to have her education in England. She was in my class.'

On the way back Dorothy thought again about the happy coincidence of the chance meeting with her friend. For his part, Alan was still amazed and wondered why an Indian girl had gone to school in England, a very distant land and for him the end of the world. So when he got home with Dorothy, he went at once to find his mother and tell her what had happened.

'Do you know, mummy, we went to the bazaar and there Miss Ollis met a school friend.'

'Really? How very nice for her to find a friend here. I'm glad for her sake.'

## Chapter 17

'She had on a beautiful blue sari. Why don't you sometimes put on a sari?'

'Because I'm English, my dear. Only Indian ladies wear a sari. Is this lady Indian?'

'Oh yes, mummy.'

On learning this piece of information, Marian did not wish to show her disquiet to Alan and changed the subject.

Later on, Marian found the chance to be alone with Dorothy and broach the matter again. She said to her, 'Alan tells me that you have met an Indian friend.'

'Yes, she was my best friend at school in Croydon.'

Marian pressed on, 'But do you know that friendships between English and Indians are not looked on with a favourable eye here?'

'I don't know anything about that. But I don't want to lose a friend found again so unexpectedly.'

'This girl, what sort of a family does she come from?'

'The Mukerji family is Christian and well to do. Agnes did well at school and is well educated and completely europeanized. She told me she is married with two children.'

'And the husband, is he Christian too?'

'That I don't know. I would like to meet him and his family.'

'You realize, of course, that we can't invite them here. It would create a scandal, in view of my father-in-law's official position.'

'I wouldn't dream of asking you. But I hope you won't mind too much if I go and visit them.'

Marian hesitated slightly, then answered, 'No, what you do in your free time is of course your business.'

So ended the conversation, and so began Dorothy's education in the socio-political realities of life in India.

A few days later Agnes rang to invite Dorothy to tea. 'I will introduce my husband to you. I have spoken to him a lot about you.'

Dorothy accepted with great pleasure and on Sunday afternoon she went to the Majumdars'. The gentleman that came forward with a smile to meet her made a great impression on her: tall, slim, with slightly grizzled hair and (what struck her most of all) two expressive black eyes in a face, very dark and ascetic.

'So you are Dorothy?' he asked her.

'Yes, Agnes's friend.'

At that moment, Mrs Majumdar arrived and kissed Dorothy.

'I'm very happy to have you in my home,' exclaimed Agnes.

They went into the drawing room and the two friends began to exchange memories: school, their friends, the teachers, numerous little incidents, some funny, some sad, surfaced in the memory of both. Madi too took part in the conversation as much as he could. Suddenly Agnes asked, 'And you, Dorothy, have you got any sentimental attachments?'

Her friend blushed and answered, 'There may be, but it's early days yet.' And Agnes did not probe any further.

Then the children arrived, Tara and Rajiv, with their ayah. They were hoping that Dorothy had come with the English child so that they could play with him.

'Our children have no racial prejudices, and nor have we,' said Agnes. 'My husband also studied in England and got a degree in astronomy at Oxford. He's now head of the Astronomical Observatory here in Darjeeling.'

'Yes, I preferred to have a quiet life of study and work here rather than a perhaps more exciting activity at the University of Calcutta, where the climate is not too wholesome for Agnes and the children. Here we have an ideal climate and one of the most spectacular views in the world, the chain of mountains over twenty-five thousand feet high.'

That evening at dinner Dorothy told the whole family of her visit to Agnes Majumdar, and was still in a happy mood on account of the warm welcome she had received. When Liam heard the word 'Majumdar', he asked at once, 'Is that Professor Majumdar, the Director of the Observatory?'

'Yes,' exclaimed Dorothy. 'Do you know him?'

'Of course I know him. He's a celebrity in India. He's not only a great astronomer, but also a scholar and researcher. I know his wife too, a very intelligent and cultured lady. They've been guests here at several official receptions. I'm glad to hear that they are your friends.'

## Chapter 17

Marian added, 'I'm also very pleased to know that the Majumdars are so well known and important.'

That same evening Dorothy wrote a long letter to Farley to tell him what had happened and what had been the reaction in the family. She awaited his reply with anxiety. It arrived a few days later. Farley reassured her: Professor Majumdar's name is very well known in Calcutta too, and your friendship with him and his wife cannot but be beneficial to you and to me too, when I have met them, which will be soon. Next week I shall be with you, my darling, and so we'll be able to talk more calmly about the problems of social relations, which are so important in India.'

The following Saturday Farley and David reached Darjeeling by the midday train. Waiting for them at the station were Marian with the children and Dorothy. As soon as they had alighted from the train, Alan ran forward to his father, and Dorothy, who was holding the child's hand, joined Farley. The young couple flung their arms round each other. The happiness at meeting was general, and they all made their way to the carriage that was waiting for them outside the station. When the luggage was loaded, Farley said, 'Dorothy and I would like to walk, and you will have more room in the carriage. You go on ahead and we shall catch you up.'

Farley knew Darjeeling quite well, as he had been there in previous years.

As they walked, the couple stopped several times to admire the view and the peaks of the highest mountains sparkling in the sun. A cool breeze was blowing and it was pleasant to be together arm in arm. Dorothy asked Farley, 'Was it very hot in Calcutta? How have you been spending your free time, after we left?'

'Yes, it's already very hot in Calcutta and, as I have already written to you, I haven't had much free time these days, as the University has taken all my time. I went to the club once or twice for a swim and dinner. Last week, I haven't had time to tell you this, I went with a colleague, Holden, to the Headquarters of the Calcutta Light Horse to enquire about joining the regiment.'

Dorothy was at once alarmed. 'But do you want to leave the university and enrol? I don't understand.'

# The Queen of The Hills

'No, no. Have no fear. It's only a simple way to get a bit of riding, leaving the horse I've bought with the army, who will feed it and look after it. It's a part time occupation that won't take up too much of my time and will enable me to keep a horse, which is very useful here and which I couldn't maintain otherwise.'

There was also another consideration in Farley's mind to induce him to enrol, which he had not yet revealed to Dorothy, and which he spoke about now. 'We don't know how the war in Europe will go, and there is no end in sight. It therefore behoves every Briton, above all in a country like India, where we are very vulnerable, to prepare himself with military training.'

Dorothy accepted the explanation, which however did not reassure her one whit. Farley also told her that he had received a letter from home, which spoke of several dear friends of his who were fighting in France; one had been wounded and another reported missing. This, obviously depressed him very much.

Meanwhile as they talked, they reached Government House.

# Chapter 18

The onset of the monsoon, in spite of being an annual event occurring on about the 20 June, is quite dramatic. It comes from the Indian Ocean and takes about a week to pass from the island of Ceylon (as it was then called) to the Himalayas. So every year it is possible to predict, more or less precisely, the date of its arrival in each particular place. After the winter and spring, when little rain falls, the first sign of the imminence of the monsoon is the intolerably hot and heavy weather in Calcutta, where the temperature goes up to fifty degrees or more; in Darjeeling however it only feels as if a storm is approaching. Then piles of black clouds build up to the south; a solid wall that advances inexorably across India. It strikes the slopes of the Himalayas with particular fury. People remember that once there fell on Darjeeling eighty centimetres of rain in twenty-four hours.

That weekend at the end of May when Farley and David arrived in Darjeeling, the weather was magnificent, and everyone made the most of it. Poor David had to return to Calcutta the following Monday. Farley, however, was on holiday and could stay in Darjeeling till early July, when the monsoon term began.

Gwendolyn took advantage of a moment's silence in the general conversation to ask Farley and Dorothy when they would be able to speak to her in private. Noticing a look of surprise on the faces of the rest of the family, Gwendolyn added slyly, 'Nothing to do with you!' and said nothing else.

Dorothy replied, 'When you want, Gwendolyn. This afternoon after tea?'

So after tea Gwendolyn, Farley and Dorothy went out into the garden, followed by the curious eyes of the others, and sat down on a shady bench.

Gwendolyn said, 'My dears, you must have realized what I want to talk to you about – your engagement.'

Farley and Dorothy looked at each other in silence, holding hands.

'Have you thought about when you would like to arrange the party for this occasion? I think it would be best to fix a date in the second half of June before the monsoon arrives, as Farley will have to return to Calcutta early in July. That's what I think. We can think about the details later.'

Farley answered, 'I am very happy to go along with any date before my return to the University. And what do you say, Dorothy?'

'I agree with Farley.'

Gwendolyn went on, 'I will have a look in my diary to see when my husband and David are available.'

They went in doors to give the whole family the good news.

Marian exclaimed, 'I thought that something of the sort was in the wind. I congratulate you and hope that it won't be long before we celebrate your engagement. We'll have a splendid party, mamma, won't we?'

At the word 'party' Alan, who seemed before not to be taking much notice of the conversation, perked up and said, 'Yes, we'll have a lovely party in the garden with lots of lights.'

'If there are lights,' objected Marian not very seriously, 'it will already be night and long past your bedtime.'

'Oh no, mummy! Can't I stay up to see the lights?'

'If you are very good.'

At these words, Alan said no more, chewing them over. In the meantime Gwendolyn had come back with the diary which she was studying. Then she said, 'David, when do you get back here again?'

'On Saturday 24 June by the midday train.'

'Then the party will be that very evening. Let's hope that we can have it in the open. But we must bear in mind that the monsoon may arrive before that. We'll get everything ready for a party in the garden or in the house. We'll make the final decision when we know exactly where the monsoon has got to.'

'That's fine,' said Dorothy, who was rather in the dark about Gwendolyn's preoccupation with the monsoon, but she was full of admiration for her ability to arrange everything in very little time. 'I shall be pleased if David can be here too.'

A few days later invitations for the party were sent out, limited to a few persons: the Governor and his wife and the Waterhouses naturally,

## Chapter 18

Dr Andrews, the Majumdar family, the Vicar and his wife, and Mr and Mrs Starkie. This last gentleman was a friend and university colleague who, like Farley, was spending the vacation in Darjeeling – a score of guests in all.

On Saturday Farley and Dorothy rode down the Lebong, the military base where Dr Andrews worked, to take him his invitation by hand. Dr Andrews, who had been told by telephone that they were coming, was waiting for them. It was a joyful reunion.

'I am very happy for you,' said the doctor, 'a very agreeable outcome that I envisaged even when we were on the *Simla*. I didn't imagine, however, that you were in Darjeeling. Otherwise I would have come myself to greet you and meet the Waterhouses.'

'Yes,' said Farley. 'We've been here a week. Dorothy and the family preceded me, and I joined them at the end of my term to enjoy the holiday.'

'So, Dorothy has learnt to ride.'

'I'm learning,' replied Dorothy, 'but I'm not yet too confident.'

'Here it's essential to be able to ride, because otherwise it's difficult to get around. I would like to show you round our camp and introduce you to my colleagues. You will of course stay to lunch. Then we shall have the whole day free.'

'It would be a pleasure,' they answered.

Now there came in a servant with refreshing drinks. He was short, a man of the hills, slim, with a dark and rough skin and eyes that were lively and smiling. On his head he was wearing a large white turban and he had on a blue uniform with a long tunic.

'This is Ghopal, my valuable aide.'

Farley said something to him in Hindi, but Ghopal did not understand, and so Dr Andrews translated for him. Ghopal's smile broadened and he bowed low, joining his palms together, and withdrew.

Dorothy was surprised and asked, 'What language does he speak?'

The doctor answered, 'Ghopal comes from Nepal, like many of the inhabitants of Darjeeling, and speaks the language of his country.'

When the guests had rested awhile and had their drink, Dr Andrews took them on a visit round the camp.

They were invited to lunch, as was the custom, by the base commander, Colonel Buckland. Dorothy was a little embarrassed, because she was afraid she would be the only lady present. The doctor said to her, 'Don't worry. There are other ladies.' And as always, he managed to reassure her.

The other ladies, wives of the more senior officers, were somewhat advanced in years, and so the younger officers were all agog to be introduced to the charming guest: Dorothy, a lovely girl among so many men, made quite a stir. She could not disguise her pleasure at feeling herself the centre of attraction, and Farley was just a bit jealous!

At the end of the lunch Dorothy and Farley took leave of the colonel and the other officers, thanking them for their warm welcome. Dr Andrews, who wanted to enjoy their company for a little longer, decided to see them part of the way home. As they rode, they chatted.

Dorothy said, 'I did not expect to find such luxury and elegance in a military establishment. The lunch was delicious and the officers seemed to have walked straight out of a fashion parade. Is it always like that?'

Dr Andrews laughed. 'It's always like that in India. The pomp and circumstance is laid on deliberately to impress the natives, who must be overawed by our magnificence. I can't say if the trick works or not. But I have to add that the young officers, so elegant in their well ironed uniforms, have a hard job to make both ends meet, as their pay is so miserable.'

Dorothy asked, 'How do they manage if they get married?'

'They don't, until they get a bit of promotion and so have a slightly higher salary, unless they find a wife rich enough to solve their problems.'

Dorothy commented, 'It's just as well that you're not a soldier, Farley.'

After which quip, Dr Andrews, in a good mood, said goodbye and turned his horse round to return to the camp. Dorothy and Farley rode on back to Darjeeling.

Chapter 19

During the following days Dorothy could not always be with Farley. He, being on holiday, did not have much to do, but she had the daily duty of looking after Alan. Nevertheless, as the schools were closed for the holidays and as outside the weather was perfect, Dorothy and Alan did not stick strictly to school studies – reading, writing and arithmetic – but with the approval of Gwendolyn and Marian, they would leave the house and go for walks in the town or elsewhere. Farley went with them on these outings, as he knew Darjeeling and could take them to the best places. Alan had been to Darjeeling in the previous years, but he was too small to remember it well. Besides, Alan liked Farley; he was used to the stiffness and military formality of his father. Farley's free and easy ways were a new and agreeable experience for the child.

Though Darjeeling was only a small hill station, there were many things to see there. Quite near Government House there were the Botanical Gardens, where the experts had made efforts to create a brave show of European and Asiatic plants. Here all three of them learnt a lot from the well trained and willing gardeners. In the town centre there was the Gymkhana Club, a place where the English met socially and where there was a roller skating rink. Alan could not wait to put on the skates, and the adults had no choice but to take him. Farley had tried once two years before, but for Dorothy it was a new experience, very amusing, but also not without its dangers for novices. Naturally Alan learnt much more quickly than Farley or Dorothy. When he fell it was less painful for him, as he was already nearer the floor.

On other occasions it was the Darjeeling bazaar with its fascination and mixture of races and culture that attracted them.

But there were two special trips, each lasting a day, that Alan and Dorothy never forgot, although these were repeated several times in subsequent years.

The first was made on foot. Farley, Dorothy and Alan left early in the morning taking a picnic with them. The destination was the reservoir in the hills above Darjeeling that supplied the town with water and which lay in a hollow, surrounded by woods, a very quiet and romantic place. But what impressed Alan most was that, to get there, you had to cross bridges that carried the water pipes from the reservoir to Darjeeling over ravines which were often deep. Alan was nervous at the sight of them, and in future this walk for him was always called the Dangerous Bridges Walk. In reality the bridges were not dangerous, because there was a walkway beside the pipes, but Alan liked the name.

The second outing was even longer, so it was done on horseback. Alan too had his little pony. The destination was the so-called Tiger Hill. However there were no tigers; perhaps there had been at one time. The top, nine miles from Darjeeling and two thousand feet higher, is capped by an observatory with a telescope. But for the normal visitor, like our three Englishmen, there was one thing that Dorothy made sure of saying to Alan before setting out and also on the way:

'When we're on Tiger Hill, Alan, we'll be able to see Everest, the highest mountain in the world. You can't see it from Darjeeling, which isn't high enough, but from Tiger Hill you can. It's a long way away, and you need fine weather, such as we've got today.'

Farley added, 'Yes, I think we're going to be lucky today. You know, Alan, I've been to Darjeeling two or three times, but I've never been up here to Tiger Hill and I've never seen Everest. I can't wait to see it.'

Soon afterwards the path made a final turn and the three riders were on the top.

'There it is,' Farley called out, as soon as he was off his horse, and pointed at a distant peak that stood out from the mountains to the north of Darjeeling.

'Where?' exclaimed Alan, 'I can't see anything.'

'There,' said Dorothy, pointing at the peak with her arm at eye level for the boy. 'That peak you can see sticking out behind that sort of saddle covered in snow.'

'That?' asked Alan incredulously. 'How can that be higher than our Kanchenjunga here?' And he pointed at the superb mountain which is the culminating point of the chain in front of Darjeeling.

## Chapter 19

Never was disappointment so devastating and total. Alan almost wanted to cry. He did not do so only because even at his tender age the stern English upbringing he had had in his family did not allow him to cry in the presence of one who was not of the family. Miss Ollis could be regarded as such, but not Mr Oates. So, no tears.

Farley and Dorothy realized at once that in their enthusiasm to see Everest they had created in Alan's childish mind the idea of a huge, fabulous mountain, which as soon as it was seen would darken the horizon. Instead, all that was seen was a very distant small white point.

Dorothy decided to do something to repair the damage.

'Alan,' she said, 'just think for a moment. Of us two, Mr Oates and me, which is the taller?'

No doubt there. 'Mr Oates,' replied Alan without hesitation, but a little surprised at the question.

Then Dorothy, signalling to Farley to stay where he was, walked away with Alan a dozen yards and said to him, 'Stay there a moment and watch me.' Then she returned to a point half way between Alan and Farley.

'Now, Alan, which of us is the taller, Mr Oates or me?'

'Mr Oates,' replied Alan hesitating slightly.

'Look hard at our two heads. Which of the two seems to stick up more?'

'Yours, Miss Ollis.'

'Quite right. I seem to you to be taller because I am nearer to you. But you know perfectly well that Mr Oates is always taller than I. I've told you that Everest is a long way off, like Mr Oates there. I am nearer you, as Kanchenjunga is nearer to us. And you are like little Tiger Hill, here, which is smaller than the two giants.'

On Alan's face there appeared a ghost of a smile. Intellectually he was convinced, but his disappointment lasted for a long time. It was the first lesson in perspective that Dorothy had given him. After it all, Alan returned to Darjeeling in a happy mood, but very tired at the end of the long day spent in the mountain air.

Thus the holidays at Darjeeling passed pleasantly enough, and the day fixed for the engagement party was getting near. Gwendolyn, for the love that she bore Dorothy, was all for arranging a large reception with a buffet in the garden, lights in the trees and the participation of the town band. Farley and Dorothy considered this excessive, but they did not want to hurt Gwendolyn, whose love and good will they both understood and valued. The possibility, indeed the probability, of the arrival of the monsoon before 24 June provided them with the chance to moderate Gwendolyn's enthusiasm.

So one day, when the three were discussing the arrangements for the party, Farley said to Gwendolyn, 'You know, my dear, we like the idea of having the party in the garden, but you must take into consideration that fact that the monsoon may well arrive before the 24$^{th}$, and it would be disastrous if the band were out in the rain. And we won't need lights, because it will still be daylight at the beginning of the party. Besides, they would be dangerous if it rained. As for the buffet, the few tables we shall need could easily be carried inside or outside the house, as necessity dictates.'

Gwendolyn recognized the force of these arguments, 'You're right, Farley. Very well, no band and no lights.'

On 20 June the newspapers reported that the monsoon had reached the southern tip of India. So it was with a certain trepidation that they went ahead with the arrangements for an outdoor party.

David Waterhouse was due to catch the night train from Calcutta on the 23$^{rd}$, to arrive in Darjeeling at midday on the 24$^{th}$. On the afternoon of the 23$^{rd}$ he telephoned his mother, saying, 'At Calcutta it is intolerably hot. The mugginess has already begun. I'm sure the monsoon will be here before I leave. Are you still having the party out of doors?'

'Thank you for the information, David,' answered his mother. 'We'll have to think about it.'

Gwendolyn, Dorothy and Farley held a last minute council of war on what was to be done. Gwendolyn said, 'Darjeeling is four hundred miles from Calcutta. I think the monsoon will let us enjoy our party in peace. Nothing venture nothing win.'

So it was decided, with typical British stiff upper lip, to leave the programme unchanged.

On the 24$^{th}$, the guests arrived at six, according to the invitation they had been sent. The Waterhouses and the engaged couple welcomed

## Chapter 19

them. After the introductions they were taken out straight into the garden, where the tables were already set out with drinks and various refreshments. The Governor of Bengal arrived with his wife without any formalities. They were, after all, in their own garden. As soon as he saw Dorothy and Farley, he exclaimed, 'Ah! It was you who entertained us at Christmas. Mr Oates made us laugh and Miss Ollis moved us playing a Beethoven sonata. We are very pleased to meet you again here in these happy circumstances.'

Professor and Mrs Majumdar had not yet arrived, and Dorothy and Gwendolyn were anxious to see the reaction of the other guests, all British, in the presence of an Indian couple. Fortunately they were the last to arrived, so Farley, Dorothy and the Waterhouses were able to go with them out to the buffet tables. In any case, the guests were far too well bred to reveal their feeling openly.

For Dorothy and Farley there was one worry much more serious and pressing than racial problems – the weather. While the guests were drinking, eating and chatting, large clouds began to gather in the south, black and menacing. The monsoon was about to descend on Darjeeling. Major Waterhouse therefore called for silence and invited Dr Andrews to say a few words. He seemed the person most fitted for the occasion and he had gladly agreed to do so. If he did not say all the usual things that are said on such occasions, it was only because the weather did not let him. At the end of his speech, he called on everyone to raise their glasses to the health of the young couple. After which Farley had to reply. He began, 'Dear friends ...' Just at that moment ill luck decreed that one of the first drops, a big one, of the monsoon of 1915 should fall into the glass of wine that Farley was holding, splashing his face and suit abundantly. He instinctively looked up, saw directly above his head the pitch-black cloud and went on, 'It seems to me that Jupiter Pluvius does not want me to continue.' The guests burst out laughing and clapped.

Gwendolyn gave an order to the servants who rushed forward and carried the tables inside, laid as they were, while the guests followed them in haste and without ceremony amidst general hilarity. It was all over in a moment. Everyone knew that the monsoon is no joke. The first drop falls and in five minutes there is a downpour. In fact, in spite of the laughter and chatter, there was a steady crescendo in the noise of the rain on the roof of the house, the trees and the garden gravel.

When everyone had settled down after moving into the house, Farley resumed the speech that had been rudely interrupted by the rain. He thanked the Governor, the Waterhouse family and the friends that were present at the reception. 'I would like to give a special thank you to Mrs Gwendolyn. She had been almost a mother to Dorothy right from their departure from England and during the following months up to the moment of this party, which she has arranged to celebrate our engagement.'

The guests applauded and the conversation started up again.

Chapter 20

A week later, Farley returned alone to Calcutta to resume his work. Dorothy went with him to the little station of Darjeeling. The parting was a little sad, not without a few tears on the part of Dorothy. 'I'll write to you often,' promised Farley, as the train began to move. Dorothy went back to her duties at Government House, and not even Alan's games managed to amuse her.

Now that the monsoon was in full stride, Dorothy and Alan's country outings became less frequent. Even if it was not actually raining, the humidity in the air made them less pleasurable. In any case, it was time for Alan to resume his schooling. In addition Mary was growing and wanted to be less with the ayah and more with Dorothy, with whom she wanted to learn to read and write. Dorothy also tried teaching her to play the piano. The little girl had several times heard her practising and was very interested. One day Dorothy asked her, 'Do you want to try?' So Mary, small though she was, began and gave evidence of a certain ability. Gwendolyn and Marian were pleased with this new initiative of their young governess and were grateful to her. Dorothy, for her part, was happy to have her days filled thus in Farley's absence.

At Calcutta Farley had resumed his work at the university. In his frequent letters, he spoke about the preparations for the wedding which were going ahead and the intolerable heat. The monsoon, though it lowered the temperature, raised significantly the level of humidity. He also reported a new climate of tension existing in the university, the origin of which was the political movement for the independence of India. This movement had begun before the beginning of the century but then remained limited to an ideological stance of a few groups of people without representing a threat to British hegemony. But at the outbreak of the war in Europe, which had as its battle cry democracy, liberty and the rights of nations, the Indian movement acquired strength and claimed the same rights for India too. Among the Indian provinces Bengal was the most advanced, as Calcutta had been for many years the capital of the state. It was understandable, therefore, that the university students should be in the forefront of the *Swaraj* (i.e. independence) movement, which was spreading among educated Indians. However, this movement, with a sincere yearning for freedom, had been penetrated by turbulent revolutionary agitators, whose sole aim was to foment tension and confusion, especially within the university.

Since the day of the engagement Dorothy had been very busy and had not seen her friend, Agnes, but one morning about the end of July they met in the bazaar, where they had gone with their children. It was a most joyful meeting, and the English children were also pleased to make the acquaintance of some new friends. Agnes exclaimed, 'What luck! We haven't seen each other for some time, my dear. My husband went to Jaipur for an international conference of astronomers, and I went with him. On my return I often thought of ringing you and inviting you up to our house, but how times flies. However now that we are here, why don't you come up to our house for the whole day? As soon as we get there we'll ring Government House to tell your family that you are having lunch with us and staying all afternoon.'

Dorothy and the children were delighted with this invitation, and all together they made their way up to the Majumdars'. The children ran off at once to play in the garden under the supervision of the ayah, and the two ladies seized the chance of telling all their recent news as well as reviving memories of their younger years spent in England and their common friends. 'Do you remember, do you remember?' were words often on their lips.

Suddenly Dorothy, becoming serious, exclaimed, 'My dear Agnes, I would like to know if you and Madi are familiar with what is going on in Calcutta University. I'm receiving rather disturbing letters from Farley that describe violent actions performed by the *Swaraj* movement, which is active inside the university. I'm quite worried, because I have the feeling that Farley's playing down the seriousness of the situation and concealing something so as not to alarm me.'

'Yes, I'm aware of the problem. *Swaraj* is the name of the movement for the independence of India. Madi will be able to give you more information about it, because he had kept up his contacts with his

## Chapter 20

colleagues in Calcutta University. He will be here shortly for lunch. So you'll be able to talk to him about the problem. But you mustn't worry, as there's no danger at the moment.'

Madi returned at one o'clock and was surprised and pleased to find Dorothy and with her the Waterhouse children at his house. At lunchtime the children ate all together with the ayah in a special room, so leaving the adults free to talk quietly to each other. Dorothy took up with Madi the unfinished subject of the *Swaraj* movement and its activities at Calcutta University, which is what she was most concerned about.

'It's true. This movement exists, especially in Bengal. In principle, all Indians are in favour of independence. We are too. The British Government has made great efforts to set up schools and universities everywhere in India with the aim of creating a body of educated personnel capable of governing this country. It is right that one day you should let us do so. But *Swaraj* is not a violent movement. Personally I am convinced that sooner or later the British will leave India more or less voluntarily. However, it is also true, unfortunately, that in Calcutta University there are sinister elements within *Swaraj*, and it is difficult to identify and isolate them. It is these that Farley is talking about, I'm sure. But so far they are not a serious problem. Let's hope that matters don't come to a head.'

After this explanation the conversation of the three became more general and cheerful.

When lunch was over, Madi said goodbye to Dorothy, expressing the hope to see her again soon at Shalimar, their home, and returned to work. The ayah saw to it that the children had a little rest, and Agnes and Dorothy continued to talk as only ladies know how.

In the afternoon the sky clouded over, and Dorothy thought it advisable to return to Government House before it rained, although Alan and Mary were reluctant to leave their new friends. But they submitted with a good grace when Agnes said to them, 'I hope you can come again soon and play with Tara and Rajiv.'

No storm caught Dorothy on the way home, but it broke in Government House, where Marian, in a surly mood, was awaiting her return with the children. As soon as these were out of the way, Marian came up to Dorothy and said to her rather roughly, 'I'm not at all pleased with this idea of yours. I won't have my children visiting the house of an Indian family, however well known or well-off they are. David and I want the best upbringing for them. Your presence in this house is proof of that. I hope that such a visit will not be repeated.'

Dorothy was dumbfounded at these remarks, but more so by Marian's tone of voice. Since her arrival in the Waterhouse establishment, she had never been spoken to with such vigour. But her strong character enabled her to keep control of herself and she answered, 'I am most surprised and, I must confess, aggrieved at what you have said to me. I don't know how I could have refused Agnes's affectionate invitation without causing offence. We met her by chance in the bazaar. Nor would I have known how to explain such a refusal to the children, in view of their eagerness to spend the day with their new friends. Luckily to children the colour of a person's skin is of no account, and I had no wish to disillusion them.'

At that moment Gwendolyn appeared on the scene and was immediately aware of the tension that was in the air. She looked at the two young ladies questioningly. Marian exploded: 'I absolutely refuse to let my children go to Indian houses and catch the *cheechee* accent.' (*Cheechee* is the derogatory term used to describe the accent of Indians when they speak English).

Gwendolyn, noticing the aggressive look on the face of Marian, tried to speak with the utmost calm she could muster. 'Come, come, Marian, your attitude seems to me somewhat exaggerated. There are families and families. The Majumdars are among the most distinguished Indians in good Darjeeling society. We have received them in our home and it seems to me very right and proper that they should want in some way to return the hospitality. Furthermore I must tell you in all frankness that the new generation is destined to live in a society that will be completely different from ours, one in which racial differences won't be so important. If Alan chooses his father's career, he may well find himself with fellow officers and superiors that are Indian, and so it would be just as well for him to get used to this idea as soon as possible.'

Marian went red at Gwendolyn's words, which were so at variance with what she had previously said and without further discussion

## Chapter 20

walked out of the room full of resentment. Dorothy, who had remained silent till then, exclaimed, 'I regret very much not having considered the implications of an action that seemed to me so straightforward: accepting the invitation of a dear friend. I certainly didn't expect to provoke such a row.'

From then on relations between Marian and Dorothy, never really warm, cooled further, and there grew between them an open tension, or what today we would call a cold war. Perhaps there was also a certain jealousy on Marian's side, for she was aware how happy Alan and Mary were to be with Dorothy.

Nevertheless, Dorothy took advantage of an occasion when she was alone with Gwendolyn to assure her that she would not take the children to the Majumdars' again without the permission of the family, but she insisted that this ban did not apply to herself. She also asked Gwendolyn to convey this decision of hers to Marian in order to avoid any further unpleasantness. Gwendolyn was grateful to her, and the incident was thus closed.

Every year in September there was the Puja festival, a Hindu religious festival but profane too. The English took advantage of it to organize receptions and a number of sporting activities. Among these three was a tennis tournament, and Gwendolyn, with a view to lightening the atmosphere that had settled on the home as a result of the recent argument, encouraged Dorothy to put her name down as a competitor, knowing that she was good at tennis. She was pleased to do so, as it would enable her to be out of the house for a few hours with the children and the ayah.

Dorothy won the first round without difficulty. In the second, which was due to take place a week later, her opponent was the champion of the previous year. Dorothy used this time to get in a bit of practice in preparation for this match. Meanwhile in the small world of English society in Darjeeling the word had gone round that in this unknown girl there was perhaps the stuff of a champion. So right from the start of the match a relatively large crowd had collected to watch the new tennis hopeful. And the spectators were not disappointed. The contest was furious and long drawn out. Dorothy was twenty-seven and was at the peak of her physical prowess. Mrs Tyndale was ten years older and was not expecting to meet so formidable an opponent. Dorothy's strategy of attrition was to her advantage. After more than two hours of play, Mrs Tyndale was tiring visibly and Dorothy pressed her advantage pitilessly, forcing her opponent to run all over the court. On the other hand Mrs Tyndale tried several times to shorten the rallies by coming up to the net, but Dorothy lobbed the ball over her head, compelling her by these tactics to run even more. The war of attrition had its inevitable outcome in the victory of Dorothy. At the end there was an explosion of applause, not so much for the winner as for both the ladies who had provided the now large number of spectators with a spectacle of such quality. The elimination of the champion so early in the tournament at the hands of an outsider created a sensation in Darjeeling. A few days later Gwendolyn came to Dorothy in great excitement with a local paper in her hand. 'Read this,' she said. Dorothy took the paper and read a headline, 'A new queen of the hills?' There followed a report of the match with several photographs.

There was great rejoicing in the Waterhouse household. Even the Governor found occasion to congratulate Dorothy. She alone was worried. She had put her name down for the tournament for amusement. She had never dreamt she would win it; an outcome which was now highly probable. However the date of the final was seven days after the return to Calcutta of the Governor and his staff. Dorothy could not possibly stay in Darjeeling alone.

In fact Dorothy reached the semi-final without being defeated, and then she had to go to the tournament committee to confess that she had entered it, never imagining she would reach the semi-final.

'I'm the governess of Major Waterhouse's grandchildren and I shall have to go back with them to Calcutta before the next match. So it is with the utmost regret that I shall have to withdraw from the tournament.'

The committee was very surprised when they heard this, but had regretfully to accept her decision, given the circumstances.

'You leave us, Miss Ollis, with great honour to yourself, but with great disappointment to us. We think you would certainly have won the tournament. We hope we shall see you next year.'

'I hope so too,' answered Dorothy, 'and thank you for your comprehension.'

## Chapter 20

But the chairman of the committee did not give up and asked to see the Governor. He put the problem to him.

'Your Excellency, we are reaching the end of our tennis tournament. As you will be well aware, we have in Miss Ollis a probable champion, but she won't be able to take part in the final because she will have to return to Calcutta with the Waterhouses. You could help us by authorizing the Major and his family to put off their return to Calcutta by one week, so that Miss Ollis can play in the final.'

'Why not?' replied the Governor sportingly. 'Have you spoken to the Major?'

'Not yet. I thought that you would be able to sort out the problem more easily.'

The Governor immediately called for Major Waterhouse and told him of his decision.

'I know that there is a new tennis champion in your household. You won't want to rob her of her victory. You will stay here in Darjeeling an extra week.'

The Major conveyed the good news to his family and Dorothy, who was overjoyed.

The next days were spent in a state of excitement for the semi-final. Even the children were involved and supported Dorothy. In fact she won the semi-final and prepared for the decisive match.

On the day of the final, a Saturday afternoon, the public filled the spectators area. Not only were all the Waterhouses there with the children, but also the Majumdars, invited by the Major. The guests of honour were the Governor himself and his wife. He said to the Major and Gwendolyn, 'Not for all the gold in the world would I have missed this match. I've managed to put off the few engagements that I was due to have in Calcutta, and here I am to watch this final that is creating such a stir.'

Both finalists went in for play that was fast and furious. But it was clear from the beginning that Dorothy had the edge on her rival and she won in the third set.

In the evening a great ball took place, during which the Governor presented the prizes to the winners. Dorothy received a magnificent silver sugar bowl with the inscription, 'Puja, Women's Singles 1915' and a large bouquet of flowers offered by the Waterhouse family. There also arrived a telegram of congratulations from Farley, which Dorothy read before the prize giving.

Two days later, Monday, everyone returned to Calcutta.

## Chapter 21

Great was Dorothy's happiness at seeing Farley, who had come to Howrah station to welcome her and the family to Calcutta. The train arrived very early in the morning after the night journey; which enabled Farley to meet Dorothy before the start of his lessons at the University. Gwendolyn at once invited him to dinner that very evening. After that they went their own ways.

During his time in Darjeeling Alan had missed his father, whose military duties kept him in Calcutta during all the hot weather season, except for occasional weekend visits up to the Queen of the Hills, all the more welcome for their infrequency. So at the boy's return to Government House, Calcutta, there was a joyful reunion between him and his father. After the usual questions and answers on such an occasion, David Waterhouse said to his son, 'Don't you want to see the tiger?'

'What tiger?'

'Don't you remember? Last Christmas holidays we all went on an expedition into the *mofussil*. (A Hindu word, used by the British in India, to mean the up-country away from the big cities.) There some natives came from a nearby village to ask us if we would deal with a tiger that had killed an ox. So granddad, grandma, Mr Oates and I went off and after waiting a long time, we shot it.'

Memory came flooding back to Alan.

'Oh yes, I remember. Mummy and Miss Ollis stayed in the camp to look after Mary and me.'

'That's right. And you asked where the tiger was. Do you remember what I answered?'

Alan did not remember and his father went on, 'I said it would be taken away and skinned to make a carpet for us.'

With growing excitement Alan said, 'Have you got it? Is it here?'

'Yes. Do you want to see it?'

'Yes, yes! Where, where?' asked Alan jumping up and down.

'On the drawing room floor.'

Alan went running off joyfully but was back again in quarter of a minute, screaming his head off in terror.

'Alan, what's the matter?' cried his father, running up to him to comfort him.

'The tiger tried to bite my foot off. Oh! Oh!'

The fact was that Alan had only seen pictures of tigers before and had no idea how big they were. Even to adults tigers are large and look dangerous. How much more so to a small boy! We do not know what Alan was expecting to see. What he saw was the huge beast's skin spread-eagled over the floor, its head intact, its jaws wide open with gleaming teeth ready to bite off his foot as he ran up to it incautiously.

'Come, come,' said his father. 'There's nothing to be afraid of. Will you come back and look at the tiger if I come with you?'

Alan did not know whether to agree, so his father took him by the hand and together they went into the drawing room. While Alan remained at a safe distance, his father went up to the tiger, sat down on the floor beside the head, put his hand in the open mouth, and then his head. From this slightly ridiculous and unbecoming position, he spoke to Alan, who stood near the door, appalled at this performance. 'You see, it's not real. The head is stuffed and quite dead. There's no danger. Do you want to try?'

But Alan shook his head, unconvinced. He quickly got over his initial terror, but while he remained in Calcutta, he never went into the drawing room without walking warily in a large circle round the tiger carpet.

That evening at dinner there was a general exchange of news. The major gave a vivid account of the clash between Dorothy and Mrs Tyndale on the tennis court.

'How do you know all that?' protested Dorothy. 'You weren't there.'

'Oh, I know all right,' replied the Major. 'You became famous when you won the match against all the odds. Everyone was talking about you at the Club. Show Farley your prize.'

Dorothy went to the sideboard and brought back the lovely silver sugar bowl for admiration.

Gwendolyn said, 'Dorothy is allowing us to use it for the present; after your marriage it will go with her to her new home.'

## Chapter 21

The talk then turned to the wedding. Farley explained how things stood to date. He had spoken to the vicar and the ceremony had been fixed for the 16 December, the first Saturday of the Christmas vacation. After which the newly-weds would go on their honeymoon.

'There's one problem outstanding,' Farley went on. 'Who will take the bride to the altar? In view of the fact that neither my nor Dorothy's parents can be present at the wedding, we thought we would ask you, Major, to take Mr Ollis's place in this agreeable duty. Will you accept?'

The Major was surprised, flattered and delighted at this request, and blushing gently replied at once, 'And why not? I shall be delighted to do so.'

Thus with the most pressing problems regarding the wedding out of the way, the conversation became more general. Farley spoke again about the atmosphere of tension that existed at the university.

'Nothing definite, you know, just that things are not going as smoothly as heretofore.'

The Major said, 'Blame the war. The Indians, seeing all the nations of Europe bent on self destruction, don't understand why they should be involved, and from their point of view they are right, especially as the Indian contribution to the Allies damages the Indian economy.'

'Luckily,' said David, 'these sentiments have not affected the loyalty of the Indian army. Otherwise the English in India would again be facing disaster as in 1857.' (The year of the events which English history calls the Indian Mutiny. The Indians call them the War of Independence.)

There was a chorus of 'God forbid!'

Farley came back to his worries. 'Nothing definite, I said, but minor acts of indiscipline, unpunctuality, truancy from lessons, political slogans written on the blackboards in the classrooms. The students' work suffers and teaching becomes ever more difficult in these conditions. If they get worse, I don't know if I shall be able to continue in my job.'

Dorothy exclaimed, 'Don't say that, Farley. What would you do?'

Farley replied, 'Hmm'.

## Chapter 22

Two months passed after that dinner party. All the preparations for the wedding had been completed and Christmas was not far away. That year the Governor of Bengal gave up any idea of a Christmas Gala. It seemed indecent to give a sumptuous party when all the British in India had relatives or friends fighting in France and elsewhere; quite a number had lost a loved one, dead, missing or a prisoner of war in a German camp. In addition, every day the papers published long columns of war casualties, a war which had no end in sight.

For Dorothy there was one joy. As soon as she knew the exact day of the wedding, she wrote to her brother, whom she had not seen for several years, as he was working in the Federated Malay States for the British Colonial Service. She told him of her marriage, hoping that he could be present, as Calcutta is not too far from Singapore. He replied that he was due for long leave, which he would normally have taken in England, but the war in Europe made his return home somewhat hazardous.

He went on, 'So it will be a great pleasure for me to come to your wedding and see your Farley again. He was my friend at Sidney Sussex College, Cambridge, and I knew him fairly well. A keen sportsman, if I remember. He played in the College football and cricket teams. And after the wedding I shall also be able to visit India, which I don't know.'

Dorothy was delighted and immediately conveyed the news to Farley. 'My brother, Bunny, has written to me from Kuala Lumpur. He tells me he can come to the wedding. I can't tell you how pleased I am.'

'I didn't know you had a brother. You've never spoken to me about him, and I thought you weren't on too good terms with your family.'

'You're right, but Bunny is the exception. He also says that he knew you when you were up at Sidney Sussex together.'

At these words Farley screwed up his face and tried to remember. 'Ollis? Ollis? I don't remember anyone of that name. Oh yes! I remember a certain Condell Ollis.'

'That's him,' exclaimed Dorothy.
'But you called him Bunny. How so?'
'Everyone calls him that.'
'Why?'
'I don't know. Perhaps he doesn't like the name Condell,' answered Dorothy and laughed happily.

About a week before the wedding, Dorothy was having lunch with the family, when a servant informed her that Farley's *khitmatgar* (i.e. the personal servant that every sahib has) was at the front door and wanted to speak to her. Such an unusual occurrence aroused her curiosity, so she made her excuses and went out.

The *khitmatgar* said to her, 'Excuse me miss, but sahib Oates has sent me to you to tell you that he has had a little accident and has been taken to hospital.'

Dorothy went pale and the servant went on, 'Oates want to see you as soon as possible.'

The *khitmatgar* left and Dorothy went back in to tell the family the little she knew, adding, 'I must go at once to the hospital to speak to Farley. It looks as if the wedding is off for the moment ...'

At these words Gwendolyn offered to go with her, and as soon as lunch was over the two friends left.

The beginning of a series of events at the University had been so insignificant that Farley had not even mentioned them to Dorothy. For some months now the students had become restless at the end of each lesson. In spite of an order issued by the College Principal forbidding the students to leave the classroom before the bell rang, some teachers had given way to the young men's impatience. This was one among many symptoms of the indiscipline in college. As it was always hot in Calcutta, it was almost essential that the classroom doors should stay open for ventilation. So the students that came out early and walked down the corridors chatting, disturbed lessons. One day Farley lost patience, and going out into the corridor, stood with his arms outstretched to block the way to the students that were advancing, telling them firmly, 'Go back to your classrooms. You know very well that you are not allowed to leave before the bell goes.' Perhaps a few students were pushed against Farley by those that were behind and did

*Chapter 22*

not hear what he was saying. At all events the young men obeyed for the moment. However in the overheated psychological atmosphere that existed in the college, the incident was exaggerated and modified, and the word went round that Professor Oates had set upon a student. A few days later, when the teacher was putting up on the notice board a list of names of the team for a cricket match (he was president of the college cricket club), he was attacked from behind by four students, fanatical for *Swaraj*, knocked down and kicked and punched. The attack was over very quickly, because other teachers, attracted by the shouting, came to the rescue and the four attackers ran off. Farley was in a bad way and was taken immediately to hospital, where it was ascertained that there were no fractures and no internal organs damaged, but there was severe bruising all over, both on the body and the face. It was in this sorry state that Dorothy, accompanied by Gwendolyn, found him. She was very upset seeing him in this condition.

'Heavens! What on earth has happened?'

Farley forced a smile and said, 'Appearances are much worse that the reality. The doctor told me that the injuries are superficial and that there are no internal ones. They also took the precaution of giving me an anti-tetanus injection. Time and nature will do the rest.' He then told the ladies the details of what had happened.

Farley went on, 'However I regret that all this will force the postponement of the wedding. You will have to inform the vicar. My colleague, Starkie, will see to the rest. My Christmas holidays will be longer than I expected. I think I shall use them to write some poems. Next time you come, Dorothy, will you bring me a pencil and an exercise book?'

Then Dorothy and Gwendolyn left the hospital. Dorothy thought, 'If his mind is running along those lines, my dear Farley can't be too bad.' Which was precisely the impression that Farley wanted to create.

This assault made an immediate furore, not only in academic circles, but in the entire British community in Calcutta. In fact, Farley's injuries proved more serious than was at first apparent. The bruising had resulted in much internal bleeding especially in the facial area. A deep cut over his right eyebrow took time to heal. Also his right arm, with which he had tried to ward off the blows, was very swollen and discoloured. The doctors feared there was a hairline fracture of the bone. All this would require a hospital stay of at least three weeks.

Dorothy and the Waterhouses tried to relieve the boredom of his time in hospital by affectionately cheering him up out of the depression that resulted from it. In fact, he could not understand how a really very trivial incident had caused such a violent reaction against him. The Major tried to console him, saying, 'It's the times we live in, my friend. It's not your fault.'

When Farley was better and could return to work, the University set up an enquiry to look into the affair and to discover the culprits, if possible. Farley had also to defend himself against a charge of having assaulted a student. It was difficult, however, to find someone who would admit to having been assaulted that day in the corridor. Only one young man said at the enquiry, 'Professor Oates hit me.' Farley replied at once without giving the lad time to think, 'Where do you allege I hit you? On the head?' he said, touching the left-hand side of his own head. The young man, who was standing facing him, was induced to copy the gesture mirror-wise and touched the right side of his head, replying, 'Yes, on my ear.' Too late he realized the trap he had fallen into. Farley riposted with a smile, 'Oh sure, that might well be true if I were left handed, but I'm not.'

Other students stated that on that day in the corridor the professor had held his arms outstretched to hold back the students, as he himself had declared. Among these, however, there had been no victim of the alleged aggression. So that charge against Farley was declared unfounded.

The identity of Farley's aggressors was never discovered. But it was known that they were activists of the revolutionary wing of the *Swaraj* movement in the University; a wing, whose undisputed leader was a certain Prakash Lal, a brilliant but disorderly student who encouraged acts of defiance against the university authorities and who throughout the enquiry refused to condemn the assault. So although there was no proof that he had been one of Farley's assailants, he was expelled from the college for his attitude during the affair.

The longer the enquiry lasted, the clearer it became that the man really responsible for the trouble was the Principal of the College. It

## Chapter 22

was he in fact that condoned the supine attitude of the teachers in the face of student indiscipline, and that had made more vulnerable those that wanted to maintain the standards that existed in the college before 1914. So at the end of the enquiry the Principal announced his resignation to take effect at the end of the current academic year.

Farley, on the other hand, came out of the enquiry without a stain on his character. However it was inevitable that he should be held responsible, indirectly, for the expulsion of Prakash Lal. Farley, for his part, no longer felt relaxed in his relations with the students and wondered if it would not be better to get away from teaching for a year or two, until the affair had been forgotten. There was another consideration that influenced his decision. That spring of 1916 the British government, for the first time in the history of England, introduced military conscription to make up for the losses suffered in the war. Farley thought that he should also take a more active part in the struggle, like so many of his contemporaries.

At the end of the enquiry, which concluded with the complete exoneration of Farley from the charge that was laid against him, he began to think of the possibility of enrolling in the crack cavalry regiment, Probyn's Horse, then stationed near the Afghan border. But there was an obstacle to overcome. Would Dorothy, as a young wife, agree to move into an uncomfortable military camp to be near her husband, or would she rather stay in Calcutta?

The young couple discussed the subject at length. Dorothy said, 'This is a sad moment for our country. So many young couples are separated because of the war, so I consider myself lucky to be able to be with you wherever you go, if that is possible.'

Farley was touched and kissed her. 'I never had any doubts on the score of your understanding and courage.'

They then made certain decisions. Farley would hand in at once his resignation from the University, to take effect from the end of the academic year. Then they fixed the earliest possible date for the wedding. They thought that the Easter break would be the most suitable, for they could use the two week holiday for the honeymoon, short though it might be. After that Farley would resume his teaching and Dorothy would continue her work at Government House, but she would live with Farley in a flat nearby that they would rent furnished for a few months.

The Waterhouses were naturally the first to be informed of their plans. Gwendolyn, ever enthusiastic, exclaimed, 'At least we shall be able to hail the bride and groom after so many contretemps. About time too. Dorothy, we'll go tomorrow and speak to the vicar. Then we'll start seeing about your new house.'

Farley had in fact given notice at his bachelor flat and found a furnished flat near Government House, so that Dorothy could have her first newly-wed's house and at the same time carry on her work.

The wedding was fixed for the afternoon of Maundy Thursday. A few days before, Dorothy's brother arrived from Kuala Lumpur. Dorothy and Bunny, who had not seen each other for several years, had so many things to talk about, but what with their numerous engagements their conversation had to be confined to the evenings. During the day Gwendolyn, ever practical, allocated a job to each person: to Liam the decoration of the church, to David and Bunny the arrangements for the guests. For herself, with Marian's help, she had reserved the arrangements for the wedding breakfast. Dorothy was to see to the bridal gown and her personal trousseau. Farley's job was to see that nothing was missing in the furnishing of the flat.

On Bunny's arrival the Major wanted to hand over to him the honour of escorting his sister to the altar. 'No,' said Bunny. 'I don't want to make any alterations in what has already been decided. You, Major, seem to me much the most suitable person for that privilege.' The Major blushed at these words, but he was highly flattered.

Many wedding presents began to arrive. Among these one of the most impressive was the Governor's. He sent a magnificent canteen of silver cutlery and a tea service. But Dorothy was surprised when she opened the present of Lady Constance, the Governor's wife, who sent her an heirloom, a valuable embroidered veil. The very simple dress and accessories that Dorothy had chosen were enhanced by this marvellous gift.

The ceremony in the parish church was short and quiet, as the couple had wished. Coming out of the church Dorothy was radiant and superbly elegant but very nervous. The real surprise was reserved

## Chapter 22

for Farley, when he saw a group of university students who had come to greet the bride and groom. Two of them came forward and placed garlands of white flowers round their necks for good wishes. This gesture, very frequent in India, is one of friendship, welcome, good wishes, according to the circumstances. The couple were very touched and the guests loudly applauded this symbolic gesture.

On arrival at Government House, everyone went into the garden where Dorothy and Farley awaited the guests to shake hands with each one in turn, thanking them for their presents and exchanging a friendly word or two. The guests stood quietly in a queue to congratulate the young couple. Even Alan and Mary awaited their turn to kiss Dorothy and Farley and to deliver the little speech that they had carefully rehearsed; at the conclusion of which they offered their wedding present: a jewel-case containing the Waterhouse family's present, a very fine necklace and turquoise and gold earrings. When these formalities were over the wedding breakfast began.

The couple left for Delhi according to plan by the night train in a first class compartment. The long journey would thus be more agreeable.

Chapter 23

The first class compartments of Indian trains of the period were equipped with every possible comfort for quite long journeys. They were also of different sizes. The small ones contained two transversal bunks, one above the other, which took up the whole width of the train. The large ones had two pairs of bunks, on the left and the right. Both types had ample space to walk around, sit down, stow the luggage, etc., and at the far end they were provided with a complete bathroom with various hygienic accessories. As there were no corridors in this part of the train, at meal times one had to alight from the train, lock the compartment to keep thieves out and go to the station restaurant. The train would wait for the time required to eat the meal. So the average speed, even of 'express' trains, was very moderate. But who in India is in a hurry? This is one of the things westerners worry about, say the Indians.

Farley and Dorothy occupied a small compartment for two, not very suited however to matrimonial intimacy, and travelled that night, the following day and a second night, arriving at Delhi at dawn on the third day. They changed trains and went on to Jaipur, the first stopping place on their journey, where they spent a few days. For the young couple, more particularly for Dorothy, this was their first contact with the 'real' India. For Dorothy had always lived in the European quarter of Calcutta and Darjeeling and was unfamiliar with the multicoloured flower and spice markets, the countless huge bazaars with a bewildering array of colours that staggered the strangers. Jaipur is called the pink city on account of the colour of its buildings. The couple visited it with the help of a guide, who invited them to admire the Maharajah's Palace with its interesting museum and the famous astronomical complex built in the eighteenth century by Maharajah Sawai Jai Singh, a brilliant astronomer. They were delighted by the Palace of the Winds and fascinated by the variety of the women's saris and the men's turbans, as well as by the colourful trappings of the horses and camels.

# The Queen of The Hills

They spent the next day at Fort Amber, a little way outside Jaipur. They travelled by rickshaw to the foot of the hill, and there the rickshawman dropped them. Dorothy exclaimed, 'Do we have to walk up there, in this heat?'

'No, memsahib, you go up there on my elephant,' said a little man in a white turban who had come up to the visitors unnoticed. Dorothy looked at Farley somewhat alarmed, but he calmed her with a look and a sign. So the three went to the elephants, which were standing on a piece of waste ground. Here they ascended a platform which was as high as the elephant's back. There they sat on the *howdah* prepared for them. The *mahout* climbed on to the neck of the elephant, putting his bare feet behind the creatures ears to steer it. At the short guttural command from the *mahout*, the animal set off with a rocking motion, following by his fellows who were carrying other tourists. Arriving up at Fort Amber, the whole group got down from the elephants and set off on their visit to the fort. While they were waiting for the guide to arrive, they witnessed a rather comic little incident. One of the innumerable monkeys living on the broad terraces of the fort scampered down on to the cart of an itinerant trader selling nuts and stole a packet. When he realized his loss he tried quite uselessly to catch the thief, yelling wildly, but of course it had vanished into the void. Everyone laughed at the incident except the trader.

Our tourists spent the morning visiting the seventeenth century palace, admiring its priceless mosaics and the play of light in the hall of mirrors, where the Maharajah spent his days. They returned to the plain on foot. On the way they met a seller of scented essences, who offered to Dorothy his '*attar*' perfumes to smell. Farley bought her the 'jasmine'. Further down the hill, they met a snake charmer with his cobra that was sticking out of a basket. Dorothy suddenly began to walk more quickly, and the attempts of the charmer to delay her were of no avail. She called out, 'I'm not afraid but I don't like that kind of spectacle.'

The following day the couple left by train for Agra. However fulsome had been the descriptions they had read of this splendid city, the reality surpassed all their expectations. The fabulous Taj Mahal, a magnificent and graceful building in white marble, remains the symbol

## Chapter 23

of love and conjugal fidelity. The Moghul emperor, Shahjehan, had it built in memory of his beloved wife who is buried in it with her husband. The Red Fort too, with its marvellous palace, gave the young couple an idea of the wealth of the Moghul emperors.

Farley and Dorothy stayed a few days in Agra. From there they took a taxi to visit Fatehpur Sikri, the deserted city, once the capital of the Moghul emperor, Akbar, abandoned after only a few years, probably because the water supply dried up. The palaces and other buildings in red sandstone, which is a local stone, have been maintained in perfect condition to this day. Here too the monkeys roam around without let or hindrance in the deserted squares.

The last port of call on the honeymoon was Delhi. Here Farley wanted to see the route taken by the British troops sent to re-conquer the city occupied by the rebel Indian soldiers in 1857. These had made Delhi the centre of their resistance. Farley had thoroughly studied the events that had given a decisive new turn to Indian history and had created a colony directly dependent on Great Britain. He wanted to gain *in situ* information that would make his university lessons more vivid and interesting. Dorothy was not greatly interested in this research, so she preferred to spend a few hours of leisure in a large bazaar, full of rich silks and material of every description. She very much admired the hand painted silks and chose a few to frame as pictures for her new house.

Another day was devoted to visiting New Delhi. Today this city is a splendid monument to the vision of two British architects, who after the transfer of the capital from Calcutta to Delhi in 1912, won a competition to design a government centre worthy of the colony that was then called 'The Jewel in the Crown'. So today the independent state of India has a capital that is a marvel of architectural harmony. But in 1916 New Delhi was one vast building site, not worth visiting by tourists, in which, because of all the work in progress, it was very difficult to get one's bearings. Everywhere broad avenues were being built, straight and impressive, government buildings and the Viceroy's Palace. All the edifices would form a harmonious whole.

At first Dorothy did not share Farley's enthusiasm for this futuristic vision. But he was so well informed and was able to explain so many things to his wife that at the end she managed to understand and admire the grandiose concept. Later she was grateful to Farley for having wanted to show her New Delhi. In the evening they returned exhausted to their hotel in the Delhi of the Moghuls.

The last two days of the honeymoon were spent in historic Delhi, a monument to the glory of the Moghul emperors, now extinct, but once powerful, enormously rich and great builders of palaces, mosques and mausoleums. Dorothy and Farley had to choose, among all those things, what it was possible for them to visit in the two days at their disposal. When they went to the ancient mosque with its minaret seventy-two metres high, they saw a curiosity in the garden: an iron pillar.

'Oh,' exclaimed Dorothy, who was reading from a guidebook. 'This pillar is very ancient and quite rust proof. The guidebook says that anyone that manages to touch fingers round the pillar will become famous. Oh, Farley, do try, I know you will succeed.'

In fact Farley did succeed, to the great delight of Dorothy. 'There, I knew it. You will become famous.'

But then a stranger, an Indian, approached and said with a smile, 'Excuse me, memsahib. I am sorry to disappoint you, but if you read your book carefully, you will see that before clasping the pillar, you must have your back to it and not your front.'

So Farley turned round and tried again in the way suggested to him under the curious scrutiny of the Indian. Alas! Farley failed the test. Dorothy exclaimed, 'Goodbye, fame'. Everyone laughed.

All that was now left for them to do was to visit the tomb of Humayun and the Red Fort; a visit that they put off till the following day.

The couple spent the last afternoon shopping in the bazaar, mostly purchases for the new home. Farley made a present to Dorothy of two lovely carpets, which were sent directly to the station to await them in the Left Luggage Office. Returning to their hotel, they were surprised to find in their room a table laid for two, where they were served a delicious farewell dinner offered by the management of the hotel. At midnight they caught the return train, as other duties awaited them: University lessons, work and a new life together ...

## Chapter 24

After a short and happy interlude of the honeymoon, the husband and wife resumed their normal activities. At the University Farley found the atmosphere seemingly more relaxed and calm than before. He often ran into colleagues and students that congratulated him on his recovery and his marriage. His students did not seem to be involved in the political troubles that had led to the outbreak of violence of which he had been the victim. But Farley, in his heart of hearts, was not at ease and he had no regrets about leaving the University at the end of that term.

Dorothy, on the other hand, could not contain her joy and communicated it to all around her. She had taken up her work again at Government House with enthusiasm, and the children were very pleased that their teacher was back. Sometimes, when she was getting ready to return home, Alan would ask her, 'Why don't you stay the night with us?' And Dorothy would smile, 'Because my husband is waiting for me.'

The couple began to entertain. The Majumdars were invited, for they were in Calcutta for an important astronomical conference to which the professor had been invited. Agnes had been very pleased to accompany him, as she would be able to see Dorothy and her new home and to talk about the honeymoon.

When Madi Majumdar heard that Dorothy and Farley had also been to Jaipur, he asked, 'Did you see the wonderful astronomical complex of the emperor Sawai Jai Singh?'

When they answered in the affirmative Madi went on, 'What did you make of it?'

Farley answered, 'We admired it very much, but I must admit we didn't understand very much, if only on account of our guide's limited English.'

'I should imagine so, as it's not easy even for an expert to give a clear explanation. However in my house in Darjeeling I have a scale model of it, and when you come to see us, I will be able to tell you more.'

'Oh yes,' exclaimed husband and wife together, 'That would be lovely.'

Madi asked Farley for news on the situation at the University since the nasty incident.

Farley answered, 'Everything is now forgotten. Things are calm and order now seems to reign. But I have handed in my resignation and at the end of the term I shall leave my post and enrol in the regiment of Probyn's Horse, now serving at Dera Ismail Khan (Near the Afghan border on the North West Frontier). I leave in September.

'What!' exclaimed Agnes, 'You will leave our Dorothy alone so soon?'

'Dorothy is a strong and intelligent woman,' replied Farley, 'and we have discussed the matter thoroughly. This is the only possible solution.'

'And I won't be alone,' said Dorothy. 'You are here, and so are the Waterhouses and many other friends. And then my brother is expecting me at Kuala Lumpur and this will be a good chance to go and visit him.'

'Probyn's Horse,' said Madi, 'is a crack regiment. How did you manage to get in?'

Farley answered, 'I applied and was accepted. Perhaps they took into consideration the fact that since my return to India I have been serving in the Calcutta Light Horse (a regiment of light cavalry, only part time, reserved for civilians) which presupposes a familiarity with cavalry.'

Dorothy added, 'But before all that, I shall go to Darjeeling with the Waterhouses, as last year, and Farley will join me at the end of the term. So we shall be together again.'

Soon after that the friends left.

With his acceptance into the regiment Farley also received information that quarters for married officers were not yet available. Dorothy wrote to her brother to tell him that she would be coming to stay with him in the autumn.

The month of May was without incident, and at the end of it, as usual, all the Governor's staff made ready to go up to their summer residence in Darjeeling. For several days there was a ferment of preparations. Even Dorothy and the children lent a hand, so far as was in

## Chapter 24

their power, packing their toys. A somewhat sorrowful Farley accompanied Dorothy and the family to the station for the departure. Kissing his wife, he whispered, 'I will join your soon.' The train disappeared clanking into the night.

When the timetable of his future moves was settled, Farley called his servants together to tell them of the arrangements. The listened to him with varying emotions. In general they were sorry to lose employment with so kind and generous a gentleman. But the *khitmatgar* asked to speak privately to Farley. His face was red and he seemed troubled.

'I will come straight to the point, sahib. Can I come with you when you leave to go to the regiment? I have already spoken to my father, and he encouraged me to ask you.'

It should be said at this point that one of the most cherished memories of Europeans who spent their life in India was the bond of affection between the sahib and his servants, especially the *khitmatgar*, as he had the closest personal ties with the sahib. This bond not seldom lasted for years; indeed it often lived on into the second generation, so that the khitmatgar's son became in turn the *khitmatgar* of the sahib's son.

So when the *khitmatgar* spoke thus, Farley was very touched, but not altogether surprised and after a little reflection replied to the good fellow, 'You know that I am going a long, long way away from here and will have a completely different life as an officer in the imperial army. You are a Hindu and will probably be the only Bengali among Mahometan Pathans. Do you thing you can cope?'

'I shall cope,' replied the *khitmatgar* without hesitation.

In the face of this firmness Farley yielded. 'You will have to learn to make up my *puggri*. (a kind of turban worn in certain regiments) All the soldiers in the regiment I am going to, both Indians and British, wear the *puggri*.'

'I shall learn.'

So Farley, well knowing the strong character of his *khitmatgar*, who had always been with him since his arrival in India, said yes.

The face of the servant lit up with a smile that Farley never forgot. So the two were in agreement and Farley decided that they would leave together for Dera Ismail Khan in September.

## The Queen of The Hills

Meanwhile Dorothy in Darjeeling, with Gwendolyn's help, looked for a house to rent for the summer as soon as Farley should arrive. This was not difficult as there were many houses available. In her free time Dorothy would go and arrange the furniture with the help of the ayah and the children. It was very simple but functional and Alan and Mary enjoyed themselves playing in the front garden. The house had a typically Victorian name, Verbena Villa, and stood on a little hill with an excellent panoramic view, both of the town and of the mountain chain that overlooked Darjeeling. Furthermore it was not far from Government House.

Dorothy was delighted with her choice and wrote to Farley, 'I've found just the house for us. I'm sure you will like it.'

While waiting for her husband, Dorothy remained at Government House to carry on with the children's lessons. Mary had made good progress on the piano; she was playing with charm little sonatas and pieces that left her mother, her grandmother and Dorothy herself dumbfounded. Dorothy had resumed, as in the previous year, her activity at the tennis club and was much sought after to play in doubles. The Maharajah of Kaputhala, who was spending the summer at Darjeeling, asked Dorothy to give his wife tennis lessons.

The recent arrival of this Maharajah had thrown English society in Darjeeling into a turmoil, together with its rigid traditional hierarchy. The Maharajah had obviously spent several years in Europe, where he had married an aristocratic Spaniard. He had inherited his father's throne (he had died recently) and he considered it his duty to return to India, with his wife naturally. He was quite young, handsome, enormously rich, a real gentleman, and he spoke English perfectly as his father had sent him to the best school in Darjeeling, St Paul's, an Anglican foundation, where he had spent nine years. At the age of sixteen, off his own bat, the young man had been received into the Anglican Church. Before his marriage however, he became a catholic. These conversions were sincere, but no one could say that the Maharajah was a pious man. Like Henry IV of France, he believed that being of the same religion as the circles one moved in made life simpler.

Well, this unusual couple, indeed exotic in the eyes of the English, appeared among them and rented a large and elegant house with a

## Chapter 24

garden and (a rarity in Darjeeling where everything is up or down) a tennis court. The English ladies held endless discussion about whether they should recognize and receive the Maharajah and his wife; neither of them was Anglo-Saxon and he wasn't even white. In the end the scruples that these ladies entertained were overcome by curiosity and the desire to be received by this couple, so elegant and rich. The Gymkhana Club, the hub of the social and sporting life of Darjeeling, did not surrender so easily. When the Maharajah and his wife sent in a request for membership of the club, the committee met and held a long-drawn-out discussion on the propriety of admitting coloured people as members of a club that had always been reserved for whites. Naturally this debate took place behind closed doors and the committee members were discretion itself. The Maharajah however got wind of their dilemma and smoothed the committee's path by letting it be known that he and his wife would only be staying in Darjeeling for a few months. Therefore a temporary membership would satisfy them. So it was on these terms that they were admitted to the club. On one of their visits there they saw Dorothy playing tennis. The Maharajah was a good player and immediately recognized Dorothy's prowess. So it occurred to him to ask her to give lessons to his wife, who had played little but wanted to improve. When Dorothy had finished her game, the Maharajah approached her, introduced himself and his wife and asked her if she would give tennis lessons to the Maharani.

Dorothy was pleased and answered, 'I would be glad to accept your offer, but here at the club there is a professional coach. Wouldn't it be better to sound him first?'

The Maharajah replied, 'Oh, I didn't know. Thank you. We'll think about it.'

Shortly afterwards, he found occasion to speak to Dorothy without his wife being present.

'Excuse me, Mrs Oates. I couldn't speak openly before my wife. But I don't want Chita to have lessons from a coach, as that is not viewed with favour in our world. I hope I have made myself clear.'

'Perfectly clear,' replied Dorothy with a smile. You want a lady coach for your wife.'

'Precisely. I saw you playing just now, and you seemed ideal, not only to teach her tennis but also as a friend for Chita.'

'Thank you, Your Highness, for your confidence. However it would be impossible to give your wife lessons here. The club regulations would not allow it.'

'Well then, why don't you come to my house? There would be no objection to this solution.'

So it was arranged. Once a week Dorothy would go to the Maharajah's house, she would play tennis with his wife and would stay to tea with their Highnesses. In no time at all the two ladies were on Christian name terms and became friends. Moreover the Maharajah paid well. Dorothy's joy knew no bounds.

In the second half of June Farley arrived, very curious to meet the new friends whom Dorothy had spoken about at length in her letters. He did not have long to wait. The very evening of his arrival, the young couple were invited to dinner at the Maharajah's. No welcome could have been warmer or more friendly, and they had the surprise of meeting Agnes and Madi Majumdar among the small number of guests. His Highness asked Farley of news of the situation at Calcutta University, of which he had heard much and also read something in the papers. Then fortunately the conversation took a lighter turn, and cricket became the main topic. It was revealed that the Maharajah had been in the St Paul's cricket team and was one of the best batsmen.

Dorothy exclaimed, 'Farley also played in his college team at Cambridge. Unfortunately we ladies don't know much about the game ...'

The Maharajah smiled, 'We are politely called to order, Mr Oates. We shall continue this conversation, just between us two, at some later date.'

The evening ended agreeably. The Maharani asked Dorothy to entertain the guests by playing something on the piano. Before returning home, the Oateses invited the Maharajah and his wife and Agnes and Madi. This would be the occasion of a house-warming party and would officially inaugurate their social married life. Of course, the guest list would include their friends, the Waterhouses, and Dr Andrews, whom they had invited to spend a few days with them.

## Chapter 24

Dorothy and Farley used to advantage the short time that remained before the onset of the monsoon to go for walks or rides. They enjoyed the ideal temperatures and the splendid views of Darjeeling. Dorothy was still busy in the mornings with the children at Government House, but in the afternoon she was free to be with Farley. One day they got as far as Tiger Hill to gaze once more upon the Himalayan chain, a sight which never tires. Often in their shorter walks they took with them the two children, who were happy to ask Farley all their questions. Farley tried to satisfy them so far as he could.

The evening when Dorothy presided as mistress of the house for the first time was a great success. With the help of the servants she had prepared a fine dinner on the veranda. The table was decorated charmingly: fruit and flowers created a lovely colour scheme. The guests' places were marked with different flowers.

The life and soul of the evening was Dr Andrews, who with his affability entertained the diners. He told amusing stories involving the soldiers of his regiment and finally, as on other occasions, he showed a few of his conjuring tricks, which left everyone mystified.

'What a man!' exclaimed the Maharajah. 'We too would like to have him to dinner one evening.' No sooner said than done. The invitation was accepted as the Doctor would be staying in Darjeeling for a few days. So all the friends met again a few days later and spent another pleasant evening in company.

One unforgettable evening was the one when the Majumdars invited Farley and Dorothy to dinner, and Madi was able to fulfil his promise to explain how the Jaipur observatory worked. Madi had built not only a model of all the construction on the observatory site, but also a mechanism, attached to the walls and ceiling of the room, which enabled the 'sun' to go round. This was represented by a lamp in the position in which our sun would be at any time on any day of the year. So under the guiding hand of an expert, the guests were able to understanding much better the work performed by the Jaipur constructions, observing the shadow cast by them and how it changed according to the seasons. It was a revelation of the genius of the maharajah that had created the observatory in the eighteenth century.

The summer months spent in Darjeeling were the happiest that Dorothy and Farley had had so far in their married life. But the summer was drawing to its end and the time arrived for everyone to return to Calcutta; a particularly sad return for Dorothy, for she would be separated, not only temporarily from Farley, but also from the Waterhouses, with whom she had spent two years that had totally transformed her life.

The day of Dorothy's departure for Kuala Lumpur arrived only too quickly. For his wife Farley had booked a nice cabin on the SS *Alexandra* so that she should have a comfortable voyage. She was accompanied on board, not only by Farley but by the entire Waterhouse family except for David, who was on duty. The children were in a flutter of excitement and wanted to know all about the ship. The adults, on the other hand, and in particular Gwendolyn, were rather sad.

'I hope you will have a pleasant voyage,' said Gwendolyn, 'and enjoy your stay with your brother. But come back to us quickly, for we shall miss you a lot.'

Dorothy, who till then had managed to hold in her tears, burst out crying, and only the tender strong embrace of Farley was able to calm her.

'Be brave, darling,' he said. 'It won't be long before we are together again.'

When it was time to go on shore, the children did not want to leave Dorothy and they too burst into tears, having only just realized that she was leaving them.

Both on the quayside and on the ship there was much waving of handkerchiefs as the SS *Alexandra* moved off and finally disappeared round a bend in the river Hugli.

Nothing remained for Farley to do except to pack his own luggage with the help of the *khitmatgar*. A few days later the time for departure arrived for him too.

Arriving at Howrah, the impressive station of Calcutta, he found the platform for the Delhi train. He was surprised to see his *khitmatgar*, who had preceded him, waiting with all his family; father, mother, brothers and sisters. They had come, not only to see the young man

## Chapter 24

off, but also to thank Farley for having deemed him worthy to accompany him in his new life. The *khitmatgar* was proud to introduce his family to his master, who gave them the salaam, the traditional greeting that Farley knew well after so many years in India.

At the conclusion of these pleasant formalities, the servant settled Farley in his first class compartment and returned to take leave of his family before taking his seat in the third class section of the train. It would have been inconceivable for the two to travel together. Farley's horse was also taken to the appropriate part of the train, where it would be looked after by special attendants.

The long train plunged into the night, taking Farley to his new military life.

# Chapter 25

Farley had as a travelling companion a quite elderly gentleman, with whom he held little conversation before going to bed. From what he said, Farley was able to discover two things: that although he was European, he was not English, and that he played chess; because after the first formal greetings, the gentleman had said suddenly in an English that he spoke with difficulty, 'Do you play chess?'

'Yes, I used to play at school.'

'Well, shall we play tomorrow morning?'

'With pleasure.'

After which the gentleman sank into a silence broken only by a few mono-syllables when Farley tried to make conversation with him. So he gave up, not wishing to appear importunate.

At dawn the train stopped at Benares, so that the first class passengers should get out and have breakfast in the station restaurant. Politeness demanded that Farley and his fellow traveller should go there together. At table before a copious English breakfast the stranger became more communicative.

'You must excuse me, sir, if I seemed somewhat morose yesterday evening. I was very tired and was longing to go to bed.'

Farley smiled, appreciating the efforts the other man was making to speak English correctly, and said, 'No offence taken. I was also rather tired after a long day. Tell me, sir, if it's not an impertinent question. What nationality are you? You aren't English, but I don't recognize the accent.'

'I'm Russian.'

At these words Farley raised his eyebrows. He was a fervent admirer of Kipling, and for Kipling any Russian in India was a spy for his Tsarist government, which certainly had no love for the British Empire. But Farley's reaction was fleeting. He realized at once that all that was over and done with, that now the Russians were fighting on their own soil a ferocious war against the German and the Austrians and had the British, French and Italian as allies.

Farley said, 'Do you speak French?'

'Much better than English,' replied the Russian.

'Well then, why don't we speak in French? I speak it too.'

'Willingly. It would give me great pleasure.'

So the two carried on their conversation in that language. The Russian, freed from the necessity of speaking a language he did not know well, became even more talkative.

'I am travelling in India for my own enjoyment, but my final goal is Delhi, where I have been invited to attend a chess competition for the young people of India. I have been asked to play simultaneously against ten would-be champions. It will be amusing.'

It was time to return to the train. On the way Farley was alarmed at his promise of the night before to play chess with the Russian, who was clearly a formidable opponent. As soon as they were settled back in the compartment, the Russian opened a little suitcase and took out a portable chess set with ivory pieces, saying, 'Shall we play?'

Farley obeyed. In less than ten minutes it was all over. The Englishman was annihilated and exclaimed, 'You're too good for me.'

A faint smile surfaced on the Russian's lips, crafty but not malicious. 'Perhaps I didn't tell you before that in my country I am a Grand Master.'

'I thought as much,' replied Farley. 'I wish I had known that before promising to play with you.'

'But that would have spoilt my little joke.'

'And you look for victims on all you train journeys.'

Both of them laughed heartily.

The Russian went on, 'Let me teach you some easy moves that may stand you in good stead on a later occasion.'

'I shall be happy to learn.' And so they spent several hours playing chess.

The following morning they arrived at Delhi, where the two travellers went their separate ways after exchanging good wishes. The Russian was staying in Delhi and Farley took the train for Dera Ismail Khan.

The morning after he was notified in good time by the guard that they were about to arrive at Dera Ismail Khan. Farley was wrong when he thought that the long journey was at an end. Getting off the train, he found the *khitmatgar* waiting with his horse. When he asked the station master where the army camp was, he received the answer, 'On the other side of the Indus, sahib.'

'And how do you get across?'

'There's a bridge,' replied the other, pointing in the right direction.

On receiving this information Farley hired a mule and its driver to carry the large quantity of luggage. Then the little procession set forth; Farley on his horse, followed by the mule and the driver with the luggage and the poor *khitmatgar* on foot. Communication between the three was rather difficult. Farley could speak Hindi, Bengali and a little Urdu, the *khitmatgar* Bengali and the owner of the mule Pushtu, the language of the mountain region near the Afghan frontier, and a little Urdu. When the party arrived on the bank of the river, Farley was dismayed to see that the bridge consisted of a long line of boats tied together reaching from one bank to the other, about one kilometre long. So he asked the mule driver if one could cross with the animals. The Muleteer answered with gestures, 'No problem'. But the horse thought differently. He reared up and jibbed at the crossing. Then the muleteer took control of the situation and advanced on to the bridge, leading not only his own mule, who was familiar with the way, but also Farley's horse, which he held by the bridle. The *khitmatgar* brought up the rear and was amused watching the antics of the horse. During the crossing Farley thought of the difficulty a similar operation would have with soldiers, horses and artillery ... They finally reached the other side of the turbulent river, where they saw a large signpost which read, 'Military Base of Dera Ismail Khan – 8 miles'. So reluctantly they resumed the march.

This base was called DIK by the English troops, who found the full name too hard to pronounce. We too shall follow their example. It was about ten miles from the town of the same name. It was a permanent camp of impressive size. Its purpose was to overawe the warlike tribes that lived in the mountains on both sides of the Afghan frontier and to discourage them from coming down into the plain to raid for women, rifles, cattle and food. In times of peace the base was manned by the British army sent from Britain and by the Indian army. At that time there was no lack of Indian volunteers eager, indeed proud, to serve as troopers in the Indian army. The privates and the NCOs were Indian, but the officers were British. However the first Indian officers were then beginning to be commissioned. These were welcomed by the British as colleagues. There was no colour bar in the Indian army, where everyone was serving the King Emperor George V.

But at the start of the Great War, troops, both Indian and British, were sent to perform a more active role in France or in Mesopotamia, where they were fighting the Turks. The Government in Delhi did not want to reduce too much the forces protecting India on the northwest Frontier near Afghanistan, the only one that lacked a natural barrier. For this reason volunteers like Farley were enrolled to make up the deficiency of manpower.

The trio reached the camp of DIK in the course of the afternoon, weary, hot and dusty. At the gate they were halted by a sentry who turned to Farley and said, 'Your name, sir?'

'Lieutenant Oates.'

As Farley was still wearing civilian clothes, the sentry went on, 'Have you got any papers to confirm your identity?'

'Yes, in my luggage.'

'Never mind. Will you wait a moment while I call the captain of the guard.'

He disappeared into the hut and came back immediately with a young officer and a private. The officer came forward and shook Farley's hand, saying, 'We've been expecting you. I belong to an infantry battalion, so we shan't see much of each other. Anyway, welcome to DIK. Private Harrison will take you to the quarters of Colonel Fisher of Probyn's Horse.'

The soldier marched off followed by Farley and the others. The captain went back into the hut and the sentry returned to his post.

After a minute or two the smell of horses filled the hot air and Farley realized he had reached his destination. The private showed him a door and went in with him, leaving the *khitmatgar* and the guide outside. Inside there was an officer with a large moustache, to whom the private said, 'Sir, this is Lieutenant Oates.'

## Chapter 25

Colonel Fisher rose from his seat to shake the newcomer's hand and said, 'So you've got here. Welcome. But why at this time?'

'It's a long way on horseback from the station on the other side of the river. I forget the name, but the guard told me to get out there. I have with me my *khitmatgar* and a guide with a mule to carry my luggage.'

'Where are they now?'

'They're waiting outside for me.'

'Better get them sorted out at once.'

'Thank you.'

Farley went out, paid the muleteer who left with the usual salaam and beckoned to the *khitmatgar* to follow him with the horse. He was clearly accustomed to doing this journey and knew where the servants' quarters were and where to stable the horse.

Farley returned inside and the colonel said to him, 'Sit down. Will you have a chota peg? You must be thirsty after your long ride.'

'With pleasure. Thank you.'

The colonel poured him out a long whisky and soda, very cool, and went on, 'Well then, when you got off at the station, Darya Khan, why didn't you ring us? We would have sent a car to bring you here quickly with your *khitmatgar*. By the way, from now on you must call him batman.'

'But what would I have done with the horse?'

'Ah yes, the horse. That would have been a problem.'

'It was a real problem, sir, at that so-called bridge over the Indus. He just didn't want to cross.'

The colonel laughed. 'Oh, that bridge! You were lucky to find it in place. It's not always there. In the spring when the snows of the Himalayas melt, the current is so furious that it's impossible to keep the bridge intact. So it's dismantled and rebuilt every year.'

'And how do you maintain communications with the east?'

'You have to go sixty miles upstream to where there's a real bridge. I take it you don't know this region.'

'No, I come from Bengal, from Calcutta.'

The colonel's reaction was one of surprise. 'From Calcutta! You've crossed the whole of India to get here? Why?'

'For several reasons. Perhaps because it seemed to me rather futile to teach young Indians Greek and Roman history, while Europe was crashing round our ears in ruin.'

'I share your feelings. But why Probyn's Horse? Couldn't you have chosen a cavalry regiment nearer Calcutta?'

'I had heard a lot about the reputation of Probyn's Horse. I'm ambitious and I aimed high; you accepted me and now I'm happy. After the war I shall return to the University.'

'Good ... Well, we've given you a troop of recruits to train. You are new too, but I imagine you've had some experience in the Calcutta Light Horse that'll stand you in good stead. Also we've given you an excellent sergeant, Sergeant Maidal Singh.'

'Very good. A Sikh. I know they have a high reputation.'

'Maidal Singh is a first rate man. You can rely on him at any time and listen to what he has to say. That's all for now. My orderly will take you to your quarters,' and he rang a bell on the desk.

'By the way,' said Farley, 'I've been told that there are soon to be quarters for married officers. Have you any further information, sir?'

'Oh, you're married, are you, Lieutenant Oates?' exclaimed the colonel.

'I was married five months ago.'

'And where is your wife now?'

'She's gone to stay with her brother who's working in the Federated Malay States.'

'The Government has promised us married officers' quarters in about six months time. I shall also be glad to have my wife here with me. She's at present in Simla.'

'A nice place, I believe.'

At this juncture the orderly came in, and the colonel said to him, 'Escort Lieutenant Oates to his quarters, will you?' Then to Farley he said, 'I hope you'll be very happy here. Mess is at eight. Full dress uniform. I'll see you there.'

The officers' evening mess in this regiment was, as Farley discovered, a stiff and formal affair. He found an empty place but remained standing behind his chair because all the other officers did likewise, magnificent in their full dress uniforms, waiting in silence. The colonel

## Chapter 25

came in last, and from behind his chair at the head of the table announced, 'Gentlemen, you may sit'. In the din of chairs being moved, the company sat down and dinner began. Farley found on his left a man ten years younger, Lieutenant Cave, and on his right a man of his own age, but already a major. After introducing himself to the two, Farley turned to his left to speak in confidence to the young lieutenant. He asked him, 'Is it a special occasion this evening?'

'No, why?'

'Well, why the full dress uniform?'

'We put it on every evening.'

'Really? Why?'

'I don't know really. I've only been here a week.'

Farley laughed and broke in, 'And I only arrived today'.

The young man also laughed and went on, 'It seems to be the Probyn's Horse tradition. Presumably they want to maintain the dignity of the British Empire and impress the natives.'

'That's strange. An old army doctor I know made a similar remark to me a year ago in a camp near Darjeeling. It must be true.'

The two rapidly became friends.

Then Farley turned to his right to establish friendly relations with Major Harvey.

This man began suddenly without formality, 'Are you married?'

'Yes, I was married five months ago.'

'And where's the lady?'

'She's in the Malay States.'

'Has she got money?'

'Alas! No.'

'But how can you keep your wife in the Malay States and yourself here on a Lieutenant's pay?'

'She's gone to stay with her brother at Kuala Lumpur, and I'm lucky. I've been teaching for seven years at the University of Calcutta and the Ministry of Public Instruction for Bengal is making up my salary to what I would have got if I had stayed on at the University.'

'Lucky you! You're probably richer than us.'

'Let's say instead: a little less poor,' corrected Farley with a smile, and was pleased to have made another friend.

At the end of dinner, the colonel rose from his seat and raising his glass of wine, called out, 'I give you the King Emperor. Long may he reign.'

All the officers followed his example and shouted, 'The King Emperor!' drank and sat down again. The colonel, before sitting down, exclaimed, 'Gentlemen, you may smoke.'

The formalities were over. The officers were free to leave the table, remain seated, smoke, talk, go to the bar or go out.

The timetable of a normal day was as follows: réveillé at 4, parade at 5, breakfast at 7. From 7.30 till 9 training. The rest of the day was free, but the troops could not leave the camp for security reasons. The town of DIK was out of bounds to the military. In any case the rankers' pay was so miserable that the only thing they could do was to save their money till the time came for them to go on leave.

But why was parade so early? On account of the climate. European found the midday heat for half the year quite intolerable. There was nothing for it but to take shelter.

This then was the timetable of a normal day. But normal days were not too frequent in Probyn's Horse. The Europeans had their Sunday, the Mahometans their Friday and their month of Ramadan, the Sikhs and the Hindus their Holy Days. The military authorities went out of their way to respect the religions and traditions of their soldiers. So in the regiment there was none of the tension or hatred that existed in so-called civil life.

Farley's first duty was to train his recruits in cavalry manoeuvres; to wheel in line, to charge keeping a straight line. The British military manual of the period defined the speed of a cavalry charge as the fastest speed of the slowest horse. Marching in single file, the riders had to learn to keep the same distance between the horses. Orders were given in English, the only common language.

Less than a week after Farley's arrival there was a night alarm. A band of tribesmen from a village near the frontier had made a raid into the plain and carried off about thirty cows. The tactics of the raiders were to get back to the village, distribute the cattle among the peasants and escape across the border to avoid British reprisals. They would have succeeded but for the slowness of the cattle, who did not realize

## Chapter 25

the urgency of the situation and had their own rhythm of walking, in spite of everything.

The orders received by Probyn's Horse were to intercept the gang as soon as possible and halt it. The cavalry were not to attack it, but to wait for the arrival of the infantry without letting anyone escape. When the gang saw itself surrounded by so numerous an enemy, it surrendered without a fight. There was a rapid informal enquiry on the spot and it was discovered from which village the raiders came and who were the leaders of the gang. These were separated from the rest and the British contingent advanced on the village, where it was proclaimed that as a punishment the houses would be burnt and the rifles confiscated. For the leaders however, those that had organized and led the raid, a more cruel fate was reserved. They were flogged, and to administer the punishment soldiers were chosen on purpose that came from that region and probability had a personal motive for discouraging such raids. Duty done, the troops returned to DIK and their days of monotony.

Every now and again at dinner in the evening, Colonel Fisher would invite a couple of officers, especially the new ones, to sit next to him to get to know them better personally. One evening it was the turn of Farley and Lieutenant Cave, the two officers most recently arrived. At first the colonel asked general questions on service: how they had settled into their quarters, how the training of the recruits was going. On this subject he said to Farley that his troop had performed quite well during the punitive expedition, in spite of their lack of experience.

'Thank you,' said Farley. 'I will tell my men that you are pleased with their progress. That will encourage them a lot.'

'A little bird has told me that you are learning Pushtu. Why?'

'I've always found it useful to be able to speak the language of the place where you happen to be. You never know.'

Lieutenant Cave asked, 'But coming from Calcutta you must speak Bengali as well.'

'Yes indeed, and Hindi too and a little Urdu.'

'You're very lucky speaking all those languages, Oates.'

'Lucky? Lucky be blowed! It's damned hard work!'

The colonel continued, addressing Farley, 'You've got a degree in history, haven't you? As you're the only graduate, so far as I know, on this base, I've had the idea that we might turn this piece of luck to good account. I've spoken to my colleagues in other regiments, and they're all for it. The men here are bored. To arouse their interest, do you think you could give a talk now and then on some historical subject? What do you think?'

After a long pause for reflection Farley answered, 'An intriguing idea, offering a multitude of possibilities. I'll think about it.'

After dinner at the bar, Farley took up the subject again with the colonel. Farley said to him, 'I have thought. What would you say if I chose the story of Alexander the Great as the subject of a first talk. He passed very close to this place, you know.'

'Did he? No, I didn't know. I should say that would be an excellent choice. Thank you, Oates.'

So the problem was settled. The lecture were to take place about sunset, at a relatively cooler time of day. Attendance was compulsory for the British, and optional for the Indians. The reactions of the men to this novelty were various. Some regretted losing their free time. Others, having nothing better to do, were prepared to listen to what the young lieutenant, who had arrived recently, had to say. Only a minority, the most educated, welcomed this new departure with real pleasure.

After a few sentences of introduction on Alexander and his historical importance, Farley had the impression that his audience was too passive or, to put it more frankly, somnolent, and he decided to do something to stimulate it. He continued thus: 'I have chosen this subject because there are perhaps some among you who don't know that Alexander and his Macedonians passed through this area where we are now. Historians tell us that they followed the river Indus during their march to the sea, and archaeologists have unearthed, not more than ten miles from here, among other remains of a Macedonian camp, a silver coin with the head of Alexander and the date 333 BC.'

At this point Farley paused, and in the silence a soldier, perhaps more intelligent and interested than the others, exclaimed, 'Excuse me sir, but how could ...?' But he stopped suddenly, seeing a gleam in Farley's eye and the expression of his face, and realizing that the

## Chapter 25

lecturer was pulling the legs of all of them, uttered a loud laugh. The whole hall woke up and there was a babble of voices. Some were asking, 'What's going on?' Some were explaining the joke to their neighbours and some were laughing. Farley left them to it, and only when silence was restored did he continue with the story of Alexander, beginning thus: 'I thought you were all asleep, but I was wrong.' More laughter. But now the audience was all ears, because they realized that the lecturer was a man of wit and was worth listening to. Farley's joke on the date of the coin was a brilliant success.

After this first lecture Farley gave others at intervals: one on the creation of the British Empire in India, another on the war of 1857, the so-called Indian Mutiny. During this lecture Farley spoke about the siege of Lucknow, in which a young Englishman, his wife and their baby boy survived all the perils. At the end of the lecture the colonel of an infantry regiment, whom Farley did not know, came up to him and introduced a young officer that was with him and said, 'This is Lieutenant Cox, the son of the baby you spoke about in your lecture.'

Farley was much moved, seeing the young man and said to him, 'Splendid! I imagine your father was also in the army and that you have maintained an unbroken tradition for three generations.'

'Six,' replied the young officer proudly. 'One of my forebears was with Clive at the battle of Plassey, and ever since then there has always been a Cox in the army in India. I'm not married but one day I hope to have a son that will follow me.'

There was great admiration among those who had heard this conversation.

The months passed, bringing with them the winter and a more tolerable temperature. Every so often a few contingents of both cavalry and infantry would leave DIK and go on a route march of two or three days, partly as a training exercise and partly to show an active presence in the region.

The spring of 1917 brought two novelties: quarters for married officers and a military aeroplane with half a dozen mechanics to service it. A far-sighted cavalry officer remarked *à propos* of the aeroplane, 'That will be the end of cavalry, at least for reconnaissance.'

Farley had been having a regular exchange of letters with Dorothy during the months of separation and now wrote to her his most acceptable letter: 'The married quarters are ready to receive you. Come at once.' A few days leave was due to Farley so he told Dorothy that he would go to Delhi to meet her.

Dorothy received with joy this long awaited letter. Her brother accompanied her to Singapore and put her on the first ship calling at Calcutta, where Gwendolyn invited her to stay for a few days at Government House. Then Gwendolyn and the children accompanied her in a carriage to Howrah station. There the two ladies took leave of each other. Gwendolyn said, 'Give my love to Farley. I hope that you two won't be separated any more.'

Two days later there was a joyful reunion between Farley and Dorothy at Delhi station. They left immediately for DIK. This time, as it was springtime, they could not cross the bridge of boats over the Indus but had to make the long detour to the north. However a car was waiting for them at the station of Khushab, and the last part of the journey to DIK was quicker, though longer than it had been for Farley six months previously.

Chapter 26

Dorothy's arrival brought an element of liveliness into the camp of DIK, for the colonel's wife and those of the other senior officers were no longer young, and the entry of Farley's pretty wife into the small military circle created a certain stir. From the very first evening the young officer presented themselves at dinner more than usually spruced up, shaved and perfumed to perfection. The colonel introduced Dorothy to the company and everyone jumped to attention, clicking their heels in greeting.

Usually the ladies, about a dozen of them, had their meals in a little room specially set aside for them. It was only on special occasions and on Sundays that they ate in the officers' mess. The memsahibs had at their disposal a cook and some local women that looked after them.

Dorothy's maid was called Asha and spoke a little Hindi; which enabled Dorothy to communicate with her. Though she was only thirty years old, she already had six children, and her wages helped to finish the little house she was building with her husband, one of the camp *syces* (grooms). One day Dorothy asked Asha, 'Do your children go to school?'

'No, memsahib,' replied the woman. 'The schools are very far away and we can't take them because we have to work. Unfortunately we ourselves can't read or write.'

'It's a real shame,' exclaimed Dorothy, 'but perhaps I can do something for you. I'll have a word with the camp commandant.'

That same evening, after dinner, Dorothy sought out Colonel Fisher and said to him, 'Colonel, I'm a teacher. Here there are lots of children of the camp workers who can't go to school even if they wanted to. As I have a lot of time on my hands, I could spend some of it giving them lessons.'

'That's a very good idea, my dear lady, and I hope other officers' wives will follow your example.'

'That would be a great help,' answered Dorothy, 'as the parents of the children also want to learn English.'

'Really? No one has ever told me about this. But it is not a big problem, and it wouldn't be hard to find a solution. Tomorrow morning I'll call together the available ladies and some officers that know Pushtu, who will be able to act as interpreters in the initial stages. Then we must find a place and equipment suitable for the lessons. So I'll get our invaluable sergeants to see to everything.'

Two days later the school opened. Dorothy and the wife of Captain Parkinson looked after the little ones and Mrs Fisher and Mrs Johnson, wife of the Major who was aide-de-camp of the commandant, began lessons with the adults. From that moment the life of the camp was transformed. In the morning, when military training was in progress, school began at the ringing of a bell and one could hear high-pitched childish voices singing songs, reciting their tables or repeating nursery rhymes. In the evening, before dinner, adult voices could be heard struggling with short sentences in English as in a chant. It was the beginning of a new life at DIK.

Farley was highly satisfied with the way Dorothy had managed to organize her days, avoiding boredom and at the same time making herself useful. In the evening when they were in their modest home under the eucalyptus trees, they had so many things to talk about. Dorothy spoke about the children's progress and of their interest in the school. Farley told of entertaining incidents in his military life and invited suggestions for future lectures that he would give.

'Do you remember, Dorothy, the lovely deserted city of Fatehpur Sikri that we visited on our honeymoon? And the story of the great emperor, Akbar, who founded it and whom we heard such a lot about?'

'Indeed I do,' replied Dorothy.

'That will be the theme of my next lecture.'

'It's a fascinating story and I'm sure it will please your audience.'

The young couple would chat for hours on the veranda in the warm air, barely stirred by the *punkah*, (a large fan, fixed to the ceiling, which at that period was operated manually by a servant) happy finally to be able to be together after so many ups an downs. And the nights were too short ...

## Chapter 26

A good piece of news was brought to the camp by the sergeants that went to the market in the town of DIK to buy the weekly provisions. They had seen, offered for sale by a dealer, an old piano that could be repaired and tuned by a private who had at one time practised that profession. This was reported to the colonel, who asked Dorothy to go and look at the piano and test it, with a view possibly to buy it. So Dorothy and Mrs Parkinson, accompanied by one of the sergeants and Captain Marrow, went off to the market. The ladies were very happy to have this opportunity to do some personal shopping: silk or cotton material, perfume and little things for the house. The two ladies tried the piano, surrounded by a crowd of curious bystanders who watched them in silence and who, at the end of the little concert, applauded enthusiastically amidst general amusement.

'Piano very good,' exclaimed the dealer pompously in his execrable English. 'All very pleased of concert. Piano very cheap,' he said, asking an exorbitant price in rupees. The sergeant got it down to a third and the bargain was concluded. Dorothy had the last word: 'This instrument won't astound for its dulcet notes in the Well Tempered Klavier, but it will play.' Amidst general laughter and applause from bystanders, the piano was loaded on to the provisions lorry and carried off in triumph to the camp.

Meanwhile the ladies' carriage departed at a much slower speed than that of the lorry, which was soon out of sight. Captain Marrow rode beside the carriage in such a way as to be able to talk to the ladies. On his right rode the sergeant who spoke in Urdu with the officer. After travelling for half an hour, when the group was in the desert between the town of DIK and the camp, the sergeant said to the captain in an ordinary voice so as not to alarm the ladies, 'Sir, I think we're being followed.' The captain looked round and saw two hundred yards behind a score of horsemen who were following them with manifestly hostile intent. Without hesitating he gave an order, 'Sergeant, ride to the camp as if there were a hundred devils on your tail and give the alarm.' No other explanation was necessary and the sergeant disappeared in a cloud of dust.

When the carriage horses suddenly increased their speed, Mrs Parkinson sat up and said, 'What's going on?'

The captain replied, 'Ladies, you will have to be very brave. We are about to be attacked by a group of ... I don't know who exactly. It's clear that at DIK the word had got around that some British officers' wives had arrived at the market and some ill disposed persons had seen there a chance to demand a fat ransom.'

'Oh!' exclaimed the ladies, scared.

'They won't do you any harm. They are only after a ransom. However you saw the sergeant gallop off. I ordered him to give the alarm at the camp and he will be back soon with reinforcements.'

Further explanations were cut short by the arrival of the gang, armed with rifles. The men surrounded the carriage, forcing it to stop, and the captain surrendered, knowing that resistance was useless. He handed his revolver and sword to the man that seemed to be the chief of the gang, asking him why he was acting in this manner. He knew very well, but was trying to draw out the discussion as long as possible to gain time. He did not know, however, if the gang had seen the sergeant make off. In any case, if the gang had tried to catch him up, they would have wasted time. Their intention was to return to the town of DIK with their three prisoners, hide them in some secure place and demand a ransom.

So they turned the carriage round with the ladies and made the captain get in as well and left at full speed for DIK. As luck would have it, the road surface was not in a good state of repair, and the carriage could not go at the maximum speed of the horses without the risk of capsizing, leaving the passengers injured or worse on the roadside; a fact which the captain drew to the attention of the gang leader, not without a sarcastic smile. The speed was reduced.

And the sergeant? He, galloping at full speed towards the camp, overtook the lorry with the provisions. The driver was bewildered and called out, 'What's up?' but of course he got no answer. The sergeant reached the camp and gave the alarm.

While Probyn's Horse was mustering in great haste to recover the prisoners and punish the guerrillas, a drone was heard and the camp aeroplane was seen to take off; the aeroplane that from the moment of its arrival had been the butt of countless jokes on the part of the soldiers, except for those few who had fought in France. 'A dangerous toy, *terra firma* for me, and the firmer it is, the less terror,' they said. Suddenly in thousands of minds the enormous and irreplaceable utility of that machine became clear, and a hurrah rose from the camp, while the frail craft disappeared into the blue sky in search of the gang. After five minutes the pilot found it still several miles from the town. The English prisoners had a surge of joy seeing the aeroplane as it went round in large circles over the group, like a huge condor of the Andes. They knew that even if they were hidden in a house in DIK, the pilot would be able to pinpoint it and convey the exact information to the ground troops. And so it turned out. The cavalry was soon on the spot, broke into the town and went straight to the house indicated by the pilot. Farley and Captain Parkinson were given the privilege of going in with their troops to free their respective wives. The carriage was in a shed so that it should not be seen from the sky; a useless precaution. Two sections were detailed off to smash in the door of the house, as the soldiers expected to meet resistance, but the place seemed empty. Farley and Captain Parkinson called out, 'Dorothy, Angela'. The voices of the three prisoners were heard replying from the top floor, 'We're up here'. The two officers ran upstairs, with their men following, and found the door locked.

'Is there anyone in there with you?'

'No.'

'Then get away from the door while we break it down.'

The lock yielded to a revolver shot, and the two couples were reunited amidst tears and kisses. It was a moment of high emotion, just as in those films which were at that period beginning to appear on the screen all over the world. The owner of the house had disappeared with his family. Captain Marrow said he was one of the gang and had probably fled to Afghanistan. It was useless to go after him. As a reprisal the British set fire to the house, which, being of wood, was completely burnt to the ground. The punishment was quite spectacular and would deter, it was hoped, further exploits of a similar nature. The ladies got into the carriage and returned to the camp, accompanied by the entire regiment of Probyn's Horse and the aeroplane circling in the sky above them. They were subsequently publicly praised by Captain Marrow for their conduct, worthy of officers' wives.

# The Queen of The Hills

As for the piano, Corporal Rogers, the former piano tuner, accomplished a miracle; what had been simply an old piano became a resonant concert instrument that enlivened many an evening for the inhabitants of DIK.

Dorothy and other ladies with the help of some officers organized concerts and choirs, especially for Christmas and other religious festivals. Even the children took part, after careful preparation, with sketches. Thus the piano became an object that was referred to with great respect.

Chapter 27

The beginning of 1918 brought Farley interesting changes: promotion to the rank of captain and the order to go to Jullundur, a fine city about a hundred and twenty miles from DIK. This promotion brought Farley no financial advantage, only satisfaction that the authorities recognized the value of his service with Probyn's Horse. The transfer to Jullundur, on the other hand, brought him both financial advantage and the pleasure of a new and interesting journey with Dorothy. Less happy than the Oateses were the ladies and officers that had to replace Dorothy in her numerous camp activities. On the morning of the departure the car was got ready in good time that was to take Farley and Dorothy with their respective servants to the station of Darya Khan, across the notorious bridge of boats that Farley knew well. The crossing was, as always, quite an adventure, and Dorothy, in spite of her fear of the turbulent water of the Indus, enjoyed hugely this novel experience, watching the skill and prudence of the driver. After the train journey the four arrived at the station of Jullundur, where the Staff College car was waiting for them. Farley was to spend two months at the College, taking a refresher course on the functions and techniques of Staff officers. Perhaps the military authorities, aware of the academic background of Farley, intended to take him out of active service and make use of his knowledge of language and communication skills in a Staff job. But this plan of the military chiefs was never realized ...

While Farley was occupied on his course, Dorothy, free from her usual engagements, could spend her time visiting the city. One morning in the market her interest was drawn to some hand-woven tablecloths, when suddenly she saw before her a familiar figure and a well-known face. The two women looked at each other and after a few seconds two exclamations broke forth simultaneously, 'Dorothy, my dear,' and 'Chita, what are you doing here?'

'We live not far from Jullundur,' answered the Maharani. 'And what about you?'

'Farley has been invited to attend the Staff College for a refresher course. He's now a captain. I've come with him.'

'This is a chance not to be missed to spend some time together again. When can you come and see us? My husband too will be delighted to see you, and we shall have a lot to talk about.'

I shall have to speak to Farley, because I don't know how busy he is or what his timetable is. I will let you know.'

A few days later there arrived at the College an elegant letter, bearing a gilded coat of arms and addressed to Farley and Dorothy with an invitation to spend the next weekend at the Maharajah's palace.

The letter had not escaped the notice of Farley's colleagues, who did not fail to rib him for a few days on his high placed acquaintances.

'The Maharajah's an old friend,' said Farley, 'and our wives are very fond of each other, as well as sharing a passion for tennis.'

When the same invitation arrived for a colleague of Farley's and his wife, the teasing and the jokes came to an end.

On Saturday morning the Maharajah's white Rolls Royce arrived at the college, and the four lucky guests got in to the accompaniment of applause from their less fortunate colleagues.

The weekend passed off happily. The hosts and the guests had a long ride in the extensive park; which gave them a large appetite. On their return lunch was served on the veranda and everyone did it honour.

Later in the afternoon a tennis match for doubles was arranged. As etiquette demanded that the Maharajah should win, Dorothy was paired with him while Farley was the Maharani's partner. The other two guests, Major Down and his wife, took turn about on the court with their friends. Of course the Maharajah won. When the games were over, Dorothy said to the Maharani, 'My compliments, Chita. You've made a lot of progress.'

Chita returning the compliment said, 'I had a good teacher'.

The evening was spent pleasantly, chatting and listening to music. Dorothy found a magnificent piano, which was not even a distant relation of the wreck found at DIK and which enabled her to perform some of her favourite pieces late into the night. The compliments were not slow in coming, especially from Major Down, who was hearing Dorothy for the first time.

## Chapter 27

Sunday was not less interesting than the previous day. The guests returned to Jullundur happy and enthusiastic about the hospitality they had received. Also Chita and Dorothy made a promise to see each other before the return to DIK: a promise which was kept, because another delightful weekend was spent at the palace.

The course at Jullundur finished only too soon, and Farley had to return to the camp to resume his normal service. There everyone was waiting for them, especially the schoolchildren. Dorothy resumed her activities as usual and made the first use of the famous piano, organizing a party for the children. The success of this encouraged Colonel Fisher to ask Dorothy to arrange an evening for the adults. Dorothy threw herself into this with gusto.

Thus without other incidents the fateful year, 1918, rolled on. One thing, however, came to disturb the perfect happiness of Farley and Dorothy: a letter from England. Farley's father informed him of the death of his brother, Frank, which occurred on the Italian front. Farley was much saddened by the news, as he was particularly attached to Frank.

From the month of September on rumours began to circulate about a probable allied victory in Europe, and Farley began to think what he would do at the end of his military service. At the same time Dorothy complained of disturbances which she could not account for; at times she felt under the weather. She went to see Dr Lewis, the camp doctor, who after examining her smiled, 'My dear Dorothy, you don't need an old army doctor, but before very long you will need an obstetrician.'

The news spread round the camp like wildfire, and Dorothy found her place at lunch surrounded with flowers. Farley too could not control his excitement and smothered his wife with every attention.

The colonel's wife was in the habit of spending the hottest months of the summer at Simla, a charming place in the chain of the Himalayas, more than seven thousand feet above sea level and three hundred miles to the north of Delhi. Here there was the summer residence of the Viceroy, all his staff and senior officials. Simla had therefore become a very fashionable town and typically English. Mrs Fisher had just returned from her stay in the hills, when she was given the joyful news that Dorothy was expecting a baby. She sent for her at once and said to her, 'My dear Dorothy, I don't think you will be able to stay here much longer. This camp does not offer adequate facilities for a mother-to-be. Our house at Simla is now empty. You could go there and stay as long as you want. I will write to our good friend, Dr Gillespie, asking him to look after you during your pregnancy.'

Dorothy replied, 'I'm all right. I don't need special attention. I'd prefer to remain here with Farley.'

But the other insisted, 'You will realize I'm right shortly. I'll speak to your husband.'

Dorothy was a little put out by the insistence of Mrs Fisher, whose good intentions she nevertheless recognized.

But Farley, sufficiently convinced by the Colonel and his wife, was inflexible with Dorothy. 'You must go to Simla, darling. You will have all the attention and company you need. The war will be over soon, and as soon as I'm demobilized I'll be able to join you.'

Dorothy was persuaded to comply, though reluctantly. The departure from DIK was rather sad, because during the time she had spent with Probyn's Horse, she had made many good friends.

On the eve of the departure in the Officers' Mess, which all the ladies attended, the Colonel offered Dorothy best wishes in the name of everyone and his personal thanks for everything that she had done in the camp. His speech finished, 'We wish you a happy delivery'. Everyone stood up for the toast. Dorothy was incapable of answering as she was too moved, but everyone understood her state of mind.

Farley and a driver took her by car to the station. They again crossed the bridge of boats over the Indus, but this time Dorothy was much calmer.

At the station the couple took leave of each other with great tenderness, but Dorothy was sad and clung to Farley.

'Don't worry, darling. I shall soon be with you. The war will be over soon. Write to me often.'

The train moved away slowly and Dorothy waved her handkerchief out of the window.

## Chapter 28

Dorothy remained depressed for the whole length of the journey. But luckily, changing trains at Delhi, she met an elderly married couple who like her were going to Simla. The husband was a retired Indian Civil Servant.

'We are happy to have you for company on this journey, Miss ... My name is Michael Godwin and this is my wife, Sarah.'

'I am Mrs Dorothy Oates and am soon to be a mother.'

'Really?' exclaimed Sarah. 'My dear, you still seem to be no more than a child. And isn't your husband with you?'

'No, he's in the army at Dera Ismail Khan. But I hope he will be able to be with me soon.'

'Well,' said Sarah, 'We can keep each other company at Simla, if you wish. In this way the time will pass quickly. We can also introduce to you many of our friends who live in Simla.'

'That would be very nice of you,' replied Dorothy.

The travellers now felt the train slowing down.

'Good,' said Mr Godwin. 'We're just arriving at Chandigarh, where we shall stop for lunch and change trains. Do you know the mountain train, Mrs Oates? It's a toy train that will take us up to Simla.'

'I know the train to Darjeeling, where I have been several times.'

'This one is very like it,' said Mr Godwin, 'but here there are a lot of tunnels.'

By now the train had stopped, and the travellers were invited to alight with their luggage to go to the restaurant. Dorothy had only one suitcase, and the Godwins likewise. So they got out quickly to choose a good place in the dining hall, which would soon be crowded. The meal was served quickly and the new friends were able to settle into an empty compartment of the Simla train.

As this train slowly left the plains and cool air entered the compartment, Dorothy's depression began to give way. Before she arrived at Simla it had almost completely vanished. The spectacular beauty of the panorama which varied endlessly lifted Dorothy's spirits, and she no longer felt alone, having found new friends.

They arrived at Simla at sunset. Once more Dorothy was overcome with admiration of the Himalayan peaks tinged with pink by the sun. A light but chilly wind gave her new energy.

'We'll take two rickshaws,' said Sarah, 'to go with you to Croydon House and see you settled in.'

'All this is very kind of you. I don't know what I would have done without your help.' And Dorothy was quite sincere.

'Oh,' said Mr Godwin. 'You would certainly have found other people willing to help you, Dorothy. I hope you don't mind if I use your Christian name. You could be my daughter.'

'Please do. It would give me great pleasure.'

While they were talking, there came up an Indian stranger in a white turban, who with great deference addressed Dorothy, 'Are you Mrs Oates?'

'Yes, that's right.'

'I am the *khitmatgar* at Croydon House. Mrs Fisher told us to look out for you on your arrival and take you to the house.'

'Excellent,' said Sarah. 'Well, you don't need us any more, my dear. We'll come and see you tomorrow.'

The friends said goodbye warmly and got into their respective rickshaws.

At Croydon Hose Dorothy did not expect to find so many servants parading in the garden to greet her: a male and female cook, husband and wife, two housemaids and a *mali* (gardener). The group gave her a warm salaam, which Dorothy returned. That night she slept as she had not done for several months, not only because the journey had tired her; the crisp mountain air had accomplished a real miracle.

The next morning she woke up in a good mood, and with a new lease of life provided by her long sleep she prepared to face the new life awaiting her.

After breakfast she called all the staff together and told them that, as Mrs Fisher wished, she would run the house during her stay, but cause as little disturbance as possible. She then asked the *khitmatgar* if the staff was happy with this arrangement. Naturally everyone willingly accepted the decisions of the young memsahib.

## Chapter 28

In the afternoon, Mrs Godwin, as she had promised, called on Dorothy and suggested a walk round Simla. During the following days Dorothy received as well several visiting cards from persons who had been informed of her arrival by Mrs Fisher and wanted to meet her. Fortunately Dorothy knew the etiquette of Anglo-Indian society and hastened to reply to the requests with an invitation to tea. Mrs Godwin was a great help to her on this occasion too, as she knew most of the guests.

During the little party one of those present asked Dorothy, 'Are you a musician?'

'Yes, I play the piano, but I haven't got one here.'

'That's no problem,' said Dr Page. 'At the home of the vicar there is a lovely piano that no one plays. Leave it to me.'

Dorothy was immediately excited at the idea of being able to play again. Indeed a few days later she received a visit from the vicar, who wanted to welcome her to Simla and wish her a happy stay while awaiting the birth of her baby.

'Dr Page,' said the vicar, 'tells me that you are a pianist. My wife plays the violin and would be very glad to have someone to accompany her. We have in fact a fine piano which you can use any time you want.'

Dorothy's face was suffused with joy, rendering superfluous anything she might say.

'My dear lady, I have also a great favour to ask you. Could you come some Sundays and play the harmonium for us in church? I hope that will be possible.'

Dorothy agreed, for when she was in England she had often played at the religious meetings of her father. The vicar's request brought back memories to Dorothy of a now distant past.

'Why don't you come and see us as soon as you can?' said the vicar. 'My wife will be very glad to meet you.'

Dorothy did not wait long before returning the visit. The vicar's wife, Margaret Parker, was still young and graceful and had a daughter of six, called Jenny. Both mother and daughter were charming, and Dorothy had no difficulty in becoming good friends with them. Margaret asked her if she could give piano lessons to Jenny, who was keen to have them, and Dorothy naturally agreed.

In this way Dorothy was not slow integrating herself into Simla society before the birth of the baby and before Farley's demobilization. In fact on the 11 November news came of the end of hostilities in Europe, and so Dorothy was hoping that it would not be very long before Farley joined her.

Farley was given leave to spend Christmas with his wife. All Dorothy's friends were eager to meet her husband, the young captain that belonged to such a famous regiment, and to discuss with him the most recent events of the war just over. So their welcome of Farley was so fulsome that you would have thought he had won the war single-handed. Farley, with a display of his usual humour, was forced to say, 'Excuse me, I wasn't the only one. I was helped by others.'

This sentence was enough to take the sensation out of his coming and aroused much laughter. Dorothy's happiness was unbounded when she saw her husband admired by everyone, especially the ladies, who referred to him as Mr 'Helped by others'.

Farley's leave was for two weeks. He was very glad to see that Dorothy had settled down so well and was not suffering too much as a result of his absence.

This was the first Christmas of peace after more than four years of war and suffering. Almost everyone had lost relatives or friends in the struggle. The vicar's wife, assisted by Dorothy and other ladies, organized a musical evening for charity in favour of the orphans of fallen soldiers. Among the various pieces in the programme there was also a Mozart quartet, for which she practised carefully as this was a new venture for her. This performance was much appreciated by the people of Simla, who had had little chance in the past of hearing good chamber music. As a result in Dorothy's mind there grew the notion that in future her bent lay in playing chamber music rather than as a soloist. Farley also approved this choice.

'It only remains to see if the new arrival will leave you enough time,' said Farley, well knowing that his wife would not lack for help; in India there is no shortage of domestic help. But Dorothy did not let herself be put off by Farley's little jokes, with which he tried to tease her. She remained calm waiting for the birth of the Baby Jesus, which would precede that of her own child.

## Chapter 28

When the day came for Farley to return to duty, Dorothy was not so happy, even though Farley kept saying to her, 'I shall be back very soon, certainly before the birth of our baby; as soon as my demobilization papers come through, which won't be long.'

At the station Dorothy, her eyes full of tears, clung to Farley, and only the stationmaster's whistle made her release him. Dorothy again became a grass widow, a term that was not too popular with her.

At the end of January Farley received his papers. He wrote at once to Dorothy, saying, 'I shall have to go to Calcutta for a few days to sort out details of my return to university life, but I shall be with you as soon as possible and will stay with you till the birth.'

By a happy coincidence the couple were reunited on St Valentine's day. Farley brought with him a wonderful piece of news. He had been appointed President of Hugli College, one of the colleges of the University of Calcutta. This was an important promotion for him.

Simla in winter is quiet and pretty cold and it snows fairly often. All the people up from the plains return there at the end of the summer, leaving only the permanent residents, who are happy to take possession again of their little town. So it was the ideal place for a young mother-to-be during the last months of her pregnancy, and Dorothy was very well aware of the fact. As everything was going normally, Dorothy and Farley continued their social life as before. Sometimes Farley would go to the golf club, while Dorothy did charity work with the ladies of the parish. Now and again they met in the house of a friend to perform good music. Mrs Godwin, who was one of Dorothy's keenest admirers, undertook to organize these soirées. The 'Simla piano quartet' had established itself and acquired a certain renown, at least locally. One day, even, there arrived from New Delhi a journalist to interview the members of the quartet, and Farley organized a little press conference before the evening concert, to which the journalist was invited. He left highly satisfied and convinced that the quartet would have a good future.

As predicted, the baby arrived on 17 April, Maunday Thursday; a fine well-built boy, fair-haired and peaceful. He was given the name of Condell, like Dorothy's brother. She quickly recovered her strength and was able to accompany Farley to Calcutta, as he had hoped.

## The Queen of The Hills

For Dorothy this was another wrench. She had the impression that fate refused to let her settle down in any one place, and that made her sad. The memory of Simla remained with her for many a year.

# Chapter 29

The links with the Waterhouse family had remained very strong during these years. Gwendolyn and Dorothy, in particular, wrote regularly to each other. Dorothy always remembered to send Best Wishes to the children on their birthdays, Gwendolyn was very excited at the birth of Condell and was longing to see him and welcome back Dorothy and Farley.

The Oateses did not to settle permanently in Calcutta, because the unhealthy climate there made it unsuitable to the wellbeing of a small baby. It was a time when infant mortality was very high, and there were very limited means of taking precautions against several serious diseases. Learning of the temporary nature of their stay, Gwendolyn had invited them to spend it at Government House, where the guest's flat was always available. Thus they would be able to be together for long periods at a time and by conversing make up for the long period of absence. Farley and Dorothy unhesitatingly accepted Gwendolyn's offer, until the time came to move to Darjeeling at the end of the academic year.

There Farley planned to take a house in which Dorothy would settle permanently with the baby and where he would join them during the vacations. Dorothy too was happy with this solution.

As soon as Farley returned to Calcutta, he took up his new post as President of Hugli College. Some of his former colleagues organized a party of welcome to celebrate his promotion and the birth of the baby.

At the end of the war the political situation in Bengal was more tense then ever. India had gained nothing from the end of hostilities in Europe. Therefore, though Farley was pleased with his new job, he felt the repercussions of the general situation. The students were ever more engaged in political activity in the *Swaraj* movement and much less in their academic studies. Nonetheless Farley managed to establish good relations with them; relations which he kept up in the years to come.

During their stay in Calcutta, Agnes wrote from Darjeeling a letter informing her friends that as they wished, Verbena Villa, their former house in Darjeeling, was still unoccupied and they could rent it. At that time the British that lived in India never bought a house but rented it, as they were always on the move. Dorothy's answer was prompt: 'Take it'.

As on earlier occasions, Dorothy moved up to Darjeeling at the end of May together with all the staff of Government House. Marian had passed on to her her children's ayah (they were now growing up), which was a great convenience to her. She quickly settled into the house which was familiar to her and in a short time she was perfectly at home in it. Farley's absence, though short, seemed to her more and more regrettable, especially now that the baby would need the upbringing of both his parents. Farley would arrive in a few weeks, when his term ended.

Shortly after his arrival he was involved in a discussion of great moment regarding the future of Alan's schooling. Every Anglo-Indian family had sooner or later to face the following acute dilemma: should the son be sent to a school in India, cut off from his cultural roots and exposed to the risk of acquiring the dreaded *cheechee* accent, or to a school in England? In this latter case the boy would not see his parents for getting on for ten years and would spend the school holidays with a relative. Alternately the mother would accompany her children and set up house in England. In this case the father would be left alone in India, separated from his family. This problem was only finally solved by the invention of the aeroplane, enabling the son to attend school in England and rejoin his family by flying out to India for the holidays.

The Waterhouse family sought the advice of Farley, whom they considered the person most informed on this subject.

Farley asked, 'If you should decide to send Alan to England, where would he spend the holidays?'

'That's no problem. Both David and I have brothers and sisters who could give him a home.'

'What's your personal opinion, Marian?'

'I don't want to lose Alan,' said Marian, flushing and almost in tears. 'Don't you think he's too young to go so far away from the family? He's only a baby.'

# Chapter 29

'Well,' Farley went on, 'St Paul's School here at Darjeeling is a very good school. While you're here, Alan could live with you while attending St Paul's. When you're in Calcutta, he could go there as a boarder.'

'Or live with me,' Dorothy broke in. 'It would give me great pleasure to have him with me.'

The Waterhouses' surprise was as great as their delight. Everyone, including Farley, gave Dorothy an indescribable look, in which the chief elements were gratitude and admiration. Before they could say anything, Dorothy continued, 'Well, it's the least I can do to repay all the affection you have shown me. Alan and I get on well together. So he won't be too much of a burden.'

Farley added, 'Well done, Dorothy. However, my advice to you is not to leave Alan at St Paul's after the age of thirteen, when he will no longer be afraid of leaving the family nest. You should then send him to a good Public School of your choice in England. The advantages of such a school are irreplaceable, both for the education and for character building.'

This compromise solution was well received by the family, who could in this way put off for a few years a more painful decision. Alan was not present at this discussion, but he knew that his fate was being decided there, as the beginning of the school year was approaching. When he was told what had been decided, he threw his arms round Dorothy's neck and gave her a big kiss.

Farley exclaimed, 'Hey! That young gentleman is making me just a wee bit jealous,' and everyone laughed.

During the following months Dorothy did not regret the decision she had taken to have Alan with her at home. In fact at the beginning of October when school began, as every year, and the Government House staff and Farley too returned to Calcutta, Alan was good company for Dorothy. In the afternoon when he returned from school, he would tell her what had happened during the day and often made her laugh with his childish stories. He continued to study the piano, for which he showed great aptitude, and Dorothy initiated him into the game of tennis. They thus spent many happy times together. Alan had a great affection for little Condell, who, accompanied by the ayah, followed Dorothy and Alan wherever they went and was quite contented.

# The Queen of The Hills

Dorothy looked after her baby personally and was greatly helped by the ayah, who spent the whole day with him. This allowed Dorothy to devote herself to the social activities she had taken part in on her previous visits to Darjeeling. The musical experience she had had at Simla gave her the idea of organizing a similar activity at Darjeeling. She found some people that played various instruments who were glad to have a pianist as an accompanist. With these she arranged concerts that once again met with success. Once again she took part in tennis tournaments organized by the Gymkhana Club, and in September at the end of the Puja tournament she won the championship; a fact which came as a surprise to no one.

During all this time her friend Agnes was very close to her and often visited her with her children, who wanted to play with Alan and Condell, who was beginning to recognize his little friends.

Agnes also kept Dorothy informed of the developments in the political situation in Calcutta University and in India as a whole; a situation that was calm only in appearance. In April there had occurred at Amritsar, the sacred city of the Sikhs in the Punjab, a massacre of a crowd of unarmed Indians by British troops to crush a supposed riot. There had been hundreds of casualties. This disastrous event had provoked a violent anti-British reaction, which had given a great boost to the *Swaraj* movement, above all in Bengal, which witnessed terrorist attacks for the first time. Dorothy, much worried by the news that Agnes was passing on to her, was looking forward to the Christmas holidays, when she would join Farley in Calcutta, accompanied of course by Condell and Alan. There was great rejoicing when the two families met, as always. Farley now had his flat at Hugli College, and Dorothy and the ayah lived there when they were not at Government House.

One evening that Farley and Dorothy were spending quietly at home, she broached the subject that was always at the forefront of her mind.

'Agnes has told me about what happened at Amritsar and said that things at Calcutta are somewhat disturbed. Why haven't you said anything about this in your letters?'

'I have also seen the news in the papers, but as the college is calm, I saw no reason to worry you unnecessarily. There is only normal political activity here, and it's kept well in hand and causes no problems.'

## Chapter 29

'I'm not a baby and I would like to know what's going on around us, especially when I'm in Darjeeling.'

'Don't worry, darling. In future I will tell you everything that happens. And while we're on the subject, I want to tell you about an idea I have for the future. Next summer the Director of Public Instruction for Bengal will be moving to Hong Kong, and I intend to apply for the post.'

'Will it be a promotion?'

'Very much so. It's a job that carries great prestige and a considerable rise in salary. Would you be pleased?'

'Yes, indeed, provided it doesn't keep us apart for even longer periods.'

'My dear Dorothy, let's get this clear once and for all. Unfortunately the Calcutta climate won't allow a small baby to stay here without serious risk to his health. So you must resign yourself to these inevitable periods of separation that don't please me any more than you.'

Dorothy appreciated Farley's straight talking and accepted his decision. When the holidays were over, she was more amenable to the return to Darjeeling with the children.

Immediately after her departure, Farley, as he had told her, sent in to the Ministry his application for the post of Director of Public Instruction. In May he was summoned for an interview. The Ministry had prepared a short list of three candidates: Francis Dunn, Malcolm Wordsworth and Farley. These were the only three that had the requisite qualifications to fill this important post. Wordsworth was the Deputy Director of Public instruction and so considered himself as the favourite for the job. Dunn was his subordinate in the administration but had already given proof of his organizing ability. Farley was the only one of the three that was not already in administration, but he had shown his managerial capacity at Hugli College.

After a long interview with each of the candidates, Dunn was chosen. Wordsworth, who considered that the promotion was owed to him, was disgusted with the decision, quit his post in the Ministry and went into journalism. Farley, though disappointed, returned to his work at the college.

# The Queen of The Hills

In January 1921 Dunn was crossing the river Hugli, sitting in a deckchair in a private flat-bottomed boat, as he had done many times before. A ship that was sailing too close produced a wash that rocked the boat violently. Dunn overbalanced into the river, and the strong currents and probably the crocodiles saw to it that his body was never recovered. This dramatic and totally unforeseen event caused general consternation and confusion in the Ministry. Without any delay they invited Farley to take Dunn's place.

Farley, who had only just returned from Darjeeling after spending the Christmas holidays there, immediately sent Dorothy news of what has happened and of his unexpected promotion. Dorothy, though aggrieved at the untoward accident, was very pleased about the promotion. She immediately wrote a letter in reply: 'I too have some news for you. We're going to have another baby. It's due in August. Do you think you can be with us in Darjeeling at that time? Condell is also happy to have a little brother and often asks me when it will come.'

Farley replied by return, 'I shall certainly be with you for the birth of the baby. (I'm hoping that this time it will be a girl). In any case I shall be spending the whole summer with you, because I shall be in Darjeeling with the Governor's staff. In spite of the monsoon, we shall spend many nice days with our children.'

In the following months Dorothy carried on her normal life in spite of her pregnancy. The beginning of June saw the arrival of Farley and the Waterhouses. Gwendolyn and Marian visited Dorothy to thank her for all she had done for Alan and to bring him home.

Gwendolyn said to Dorothy, 'My dear, you're looking very overweight and tired. What does the doctor say?'

'I'm fine. I don't need a doctor.'

'You'd do well to see one,' urged Gwendolyn, 'you seem to me much changed and washed out.'

But Dorothy would not hear of it. Farley, who came in at that moment, asked the ladies what they were talking about.

'Women's problems,' said Dorothy, without going into details. But Gwendolyn, who was worried about her friend's health, replied to Farley, 'Don't you think she's overweight and tired looking?'

The next day Farley went with Dorothy to the doctor's. He

## Chapter 29

prescribed for her some rest, saying to her, 'You can't go on like this, my dear, ignoring the fact that you will shortly have another baby. Nature had her laws and you must respect them.'

Farley interrupted, 'Now that I am here, Dorothy will obey you.'

Dorothy smiled, 'I shall obey.'

The last two months of the pregnancy therefore passed without special incident in the calm of family life, and the Oateses enjoyed the company of Condell, who was a lively boy and very garrulous. Dorothy felt herself surrounded by affection and attention on the part of her husband and friends, but she was often very tired. Early in August came the time for the birth. As this presented complications, the midwife, a capable Indian woman, thought it advisable to summon the doctor, who came quickly. The travail was long drawn out as it was a case of breech birth. It was a girl (as Farley had hoped). She yelled with all her force as she came in to the world.

The midwife in excitement exclaimed, 'It's a lovely baby girl.'

'Her name will be Pamela,' said Dorothy.

But the birth was not over. After a short time Dorothy was seized again by more birth pangs.

'What's going on?' enquired the midwife. The doctor examined Dorothy and exploded, 'Good heavens! There's another one.'

There was in fact another girl, unfortunately stillborn. The doctor and the midwife looked at each other without having the courage to reveal the sad news to Dorothy. The doctor called Farley aside and said to him, 'I'm sorry to say that one of the twins is stillborn. If you agree, we'll bury it in the garden without any formalities, but you will have to tell the news to your wife with great care so that she does not get a shock, which might inhibit her feeding of the baby.'

Farley was very upset, not only about what happened, but also about the responsibility for having to reveal the truth to Dorothy. The doctor suggested to him, 'Why not tell her that the baby has been given to a wetnurse for feeding? This would give us a little time to prepare her for a bigger separation ...' Farley agreed to give Dorothy and the others this version of the facts.

'Meanwhile, Mr Oates, it would be advisable to give orders to the *mali* [gardener] to ...'

'No,' interrupted Farley. 'It's my job to bury my baby.'

The doctor understood the strong feelings of Farley and acquiesced.

Farley laid the little body in a shoebox lined with cotton wool, found a spade and went up into the wood that overlooked Verbena Villa. There he dug a hole under a large oak tree, put the box in it and then covered it with earth. He said a short prayer and, with his heart still in turmoil, went down again to the house.

After a few days Dorothy asked for news of the second baby, which she called Joan. Farley replied to her, 'My darling, it's eating very little and the doctor is very worried about its health.' But Dorothy pressed Farley, who finally admitted, 'The baby has gone away. I have buried it in the wood behind the house.'

Dorothy wept without restraint.

As always, time is a great healer, and her sense of bereavement gradually faded. Looking after little Pamela absorbed Dorothy completely, and Condell too required her presence; he was a bright and lively boy but a little jealous of his little sister and therefore needed watching to avoid little incidents. Dorothy was reluctant to accept the reality of the fact that Joan was stillborn; she persisted in her belief that the baby had lived for at least a short time.

Little by little, however, she resumed her usual activities. She again began to arrange chamber music concerts, which were always popular. She devoted herself to social and charitable activities, and in view of her present position as wife of the Director of Public Instruction, she enjoyed a prominent position in good Darjeeling society.

Nor must we omit the additional fact that as soon as she was in a physical state to do so, she resumed her usual sporting activity, and nobody was surprised, once again, that she won the championship in the Puja tournament.

As a woman Dorothy had become more mature and more than ever fascinating and she was deservedly accorded the name of 'Queen of the Hills', a title which, until then, had been confined to the town of Darjeeling.

## THE END